"Now then," he said, "start explaining."

Blair Craddock regarded Amanda's scrubbed face and newly combed hair thoughtfully. "That smile was intended for me, surely?"

Amanda looked down at her hands, twisting her fingers together. "In a way. What's so wrong about smiling at someone?"

His brows rose cynically. "Nothing—nothing at all. Except that naturally I took that smile as an invitation. You were one of Elaine's set, at her party; your dress, your hair, your general appearance—" he waved a hand "—it was obvious that you were available."

She sat up straight. "Well, I'm not!" she snapped, anger taking the place of her former mortification. "And I'm not one of Elaine's set, either. I'm here to meet my father."

He stared at her. "My God!" he said. "James is going to have his work cut out with a daughter like you around the place!"

Other titles by
MARJORIE LEWTY
IN HARLEQUIN ROMANCES

Other titles by
MARJORIE LEWTY
IN HARLEQUIN PRESENTS

Many of these titles are available at your local bookseller.

For a free catalogue listing all available Harlequin Romances,
send your name and address to:

HARLEQUIN READER SERVICE,
M.P.O. Box 707, Niagara Falls, N.Y. 14302
Canadian address: Stratford, Ontario, Canada N5A 6W2

A
Certain Smile

by

MARJORIE LEWTY

Harlequin Books

TORONTO·LONDON·NEW YORK·AMSTERDAM
SYDNEY·HAMBURG·PARIS·STOCKHOLM

Original hardcover edition published in 1979
by Mills & Boon Limited

ISBN 0-373-02331-6

Harlequin edition published May 1980

CHAPTER ONE

'But I don't think I want to meet my father,' said Amanda. 'Not if I can help it. Do I really have to?' She gazed appealingly across the large polished desk at the solicitor sitting on the other side of it, and in the June sunlight that filtered between the slats of the venetian blind, her clear grey-blue eyes with their curving dark lashes gave away very little of the nervousness that fluttered inside her.

Amanda Dawson, at eighteen and a bit, had never had any reason to meet a solicitor before, but she had had a hazy idea that all solicitors were grey, elderly, with spectacles and a dry manner of speaking, who spent their days tucked away in dusty offices, among dusty law books. So that Mr Raikes had been a surprise. He wasn't a day over forty, had curly brown hair and a nice smile, and his office, situated in one of Exeter's most modern blocks, managed to be functional and luxurious at one and the same time, with a thick carpet and comfortable chairs. On his desk was a silver-framed photograph of an attractive young woman with two curly-headed little girls, and—so far as Amanda's nervous glance had taken in when she was admitted by the receptionist—there wasn't a speck of dust anywhere.

She had been feeling uneasy about this unexpected interview ever since the letter arrived asking her to make an appointment, and the hour-long bus journey from King's Holton into Exeter this morning had done nothing to quieten the nervous fluttering inside, but now she was beginning to feel that this rather nice solicitor might not be so intimidating after all.

'Do I really have to meet my father?' she said again,

pleadingly. 'I don't know him. He doesn't know me—he's never seen me in his life.' She stopped and a pretty flush touched her cheeks. 'No, that's wrong, of course he must have seen me when I was a baby.' Her head lifted. 'He walked out on my mother when I was about six months old and he's never bothered about me since. So why should he want to do so now?'

Tony Raikes raised his head from the papers on the desk before him and met the clear gaze of the girl opposite and he thought that it was highly likely that a good many men would be bothering about Miss Amanda Dawson in the near future, not only her father. With her white knitted jacket, its belt pulled in at the waist to emphasize her delightful shape; her shining, well-brushed fair hair; her small face with neat features and flawless skin, she might have been any one of the hundreds of pretty young girls to be seen in any one of a hundred offices in the city. But it struck him that there was more to Amanda Dawson than mere prettiness. As he looked into those very clear grey-blue eyes he tried to put a name to what it was, and failed.

He looked down at the papers again. 'You're—let me see—you're eighteen, Miss Dawson?'

'Eighteen and three-quarters. So I'm of age, legally, aren't I? My father doesn't have any obligation towards me, and I'm perfectly capable of looking after myself, you know.'

Mr Raikes picked up a silver pencil and tapped it thoughtfully on the desk. He smiled. 'Would it be an impertinent question to ask if you're thinking of getting married?'

He had a nice smile, Amanda thought, and he wasn't being patronising, or tolerantly amused, or anything like that. He was treating her as an equal. She relaxed a little in the tubby leather chair. 'Oh, good gracious no, nothing like that. Not for a long time yet. I don't believe in very young marriages, do you?' She smiled back at him, the long dark lashes lowering over her eyes and her lips parting to reveal teeth as creamy white as peeled nuts.

The smile took Mr Raikes off his guard. He nearly blurted out, 'For Pete's sake, girl, don't you know the effect it has on a man when you smile at him like that?' He frowned, taking command of himself and the situation. 'Well then, what do you have in mind for the immediate future? I understand that the lease on your grandmother's cottage expires in a few weeks, so presumably you will have to move.'

Amanda said innocently, 'You seem to know a great deal about my circumstances, Mr Raikes.'

'My firm has acted for your father for many years, Miss Dawson. He has always insisted on our keeping in touch as you grew up, so when your grandmother died recently of course he was informed.'

Amanda gasped. 'You mean you've been having me watched? Spying on me and sending in reports to my father? Well, of all the——!' Pink with indignation, she half rose in her chair.

The solicitor waved her down again. 'Please, Miss Dawson, don't get me wrong. Nothing like that at all. I can promise you that your father's interest was in no way involved with your personal life. He only wished to be assured that you were not wanting for anything in the material way and that the very generous allowance he sent to your grandmother for your care and upbringing was being properly administered.'

'Allowance?' Amanda frowned. 'You mean that my father has been sending money for me?'

'For many years, Miss Dawson. I have here'—he flicked through a sheaf of small forms on his desk—'your grandmother's receipts for each half-yearly sum as it was paid to her.'

'But—but I don't understand. I thought—Gran always told me——' She paused and bit her lip, remembering the way her grandmother's mouth had tightened and her face seemed to become pinched whenever Amanda had asked about her father.

'You must forget him, child. He wasn't a *good* man.' To Gran, Amanda had found as she grew older, a good man was someone who was a cross between the vicar and the village doctor.

The solicitor was talking again, explaining things about alimony and the decision of the court after Amanda's mother died when Amanda was only three, and her guardianship had been transferred to her grandmother, but Amanda was only half listening. She was remembering the pretty dresses, the children's parties, the dancing lessons, the riding lessons. And, later, how the money had always been there to pay for the trips abroad with school parties. She had been to France, to Italy, to Holland, to Belgium, and Gran had always made sure that she was properly fitted out, and was short of spending money.

If she had thought about it at all, as she grew older, Amanda had taken it for granted that Gran was dipping into her own capital, and she had made a vague sort of resolution that some day she would earn enough money to make it up to her for being so wonderfully generous. The idea that her unknown father had been paying for it all had never occurred to her.

Poor Gran, she thought now, her eyes clouding, it had been such a harmless little deception, and even if she hadn't provided money she had provided love and care and interest and everything else that a child needs. She had even, in a way, given her life, for one bitter cold day last winter when Amanda had forgotten to take her mac to school Gran had walked to meet the school bus, half a mile away, rather than let Amanda get soaking wet on the way back to the cottage. But it had been Gran who had caught the cold which turned to pneumonia. She had died a week later in hospital.

'—do you mean,' Mr Raikes was saying 'that your grandmother never told you that your father was sending a most generous allowance for you?' and when Amanda shook her head mutely he added, 'I think, in the circumstances, that it was very wrong of her to keep you in ignorance when you became old enough to understand.'

Amanda glared at him. 'How dare you criticise her?' The grey-blue eyes sparkled frostily. 'She was wonderful to me, and I loved her.'

Tony Raikes sat back in his large chair, realising suddenly what it was that he had already sensed about his young visitor. She had something over and above a pretty face and a delectable figure. She had a certain star quality about her. 'I'm sorry,' he said simply.

Amanda bit her lip and gave him a small grin which he found utterly delightful. 'I'm sorry too,' she said frankly. 'I shouldn't have let fly at you like that. I have a beast of a temper sometimes. But let's not talk about me—I'm sure you have lots more important things to do this morning. I think——' she hesitated for a moment and then went on firmly '—I think that perhaps, if my father *does* want to see me I ought to do as he wishes.'

'I'm sure that's a wise decision,' the solicitor said gravely. 'And now perhaps you'll let me help you? Unless, of course, you already have someone acting on your behalf?'

'A solicitor, you mean? Oh no, nothing so grand! Gran didn't have much to leave behind, you know, and she'd signed a form transferring her Post Office savings account to me. She said she needn't leave a will so long as she'd done that. She said it would make it easier for me when she died.' Amanda blinked rapidly once or twice.

Mr Raikes nodded. 'I see. And what plans have you for the future?'

'Oh, just to get a job. Gran wanted me to go to university, but I wasn't really keen and anyway I wanted to be earning some money, to make it up to Gran for all she had done for me.' She threw him a swift deprecating glance. 'Of course, I didn't know that the money had come from my father. But it wouldn't have made any difference if I had. I'd have found out sooner or later, and then I'd have refused to take it.'

'Er—yes.' Mr Raikes coughed. 'What sort of a job had you in mind?'

'Shorthand-typing—audio-typing—something like that. I finished my training a couple of weeks ago. I'm going to try to find a bed-sitter or a small flat here in Exeter and then look for a job.'

Tony Raikes looked in some amazement at this rare young woman who was prepared to admit that she was a typist, without assuming the grander title of secretary. He said, 'So what it amounts to is that at the moment you are free of obligations? That makes it easier.'

'Makes what easier?' enquired Amanda.

'What I'm going to suggest to you. I was talking to your father on the phone this morning and he was very pleased that you'd agreed to come and discuss things with me. He would very much like you to visit him at his home as soon as possible.'

'Where does he live?'

'I understand he has an apartment in London and a country house out of town.'

Amanda wrinkled her straight little nose. 'That sounds horribly affluent. Is he very rich or something?'

Mr Raikes smiled faintly. 'I'm afraid I can't answer that one. My London office deals with your father's financial affairs. But I should guess he's what they call a man of considerable substance. Didn't you know?'

'I don't know the first thing about him,' she answered shortly. 'I've never wanted to find out. He left my mother and me when I was a baby. That was enough for me.'

'But you'll go and meet him?'

The blue-grey eyes met his own eyes levelly and the arc

of finely-marked dark brows rose. 'I said I would,' said Amanda, 'so I will.'

Meeting that blue gaze Mr Raikes felt rather at a loss, which was rare for him. He usually managed to keep interviews with clients entirely under his own control. He coughed. 'Yes, of course,' he said hastily.

He was aware of a considerable sense of relief. He could have argued that it was no responsibility of his to persuade this independent young woman to meet her unknown father. All the same, he wouldn't have particularly relished the need to inform his client that he had failed. James Dawson sounded—from the brief telephone conversation he had had with him—the kind of man who didn't admit the word 'failure' into his vocabulary. And it also seemed to him that this delightful and charming young woman sitting opposite had undoubtedly inherited something of her father's strength of character.

'Very sensible of you,' he said hastily, 'I'm sure you've made the right decision. So now we can go ahead and make the necessary arrangements, can't we?'

Exactly four days later Amanda stood beside the main bookstall at Paddington Station and searched the milling crowd for someone who might be looking for a girl in a grey suit and white blouse, carrying a copy of *Vogue*. That was how she described what she would be wearing when she rang Mr Raikes up to finalise the arrangements. The grey suit and white blouse were Amanda's 'best' but the copy of *Vogue* was Mr Raikes's idea. Amanda didn't aspire to *Vogue*, normally. When she bought a magazine she chose one that was much more friendly and presented an image that seemed to be within reach. She had flicked through the glossy pages of *Vogue* when she bought it and smothered a giggle at the thought of herself wearing clothes like those featured within—or looking in the least like the model girls wearing them.

Then she had looked again and decided that they really were rather gorgeous. And no less gorgeous were the shadowy men in the background, dark and brooding and sexy. She wondered if men like that really existed. In magazines, of course. In films and TV dramas. But not, surely, in the world of everyday.

'Would it be Miss Dawson?'

Amanda looked round to see a stubby little man with short-cropped sandy hair standing beside her. He was wearing navy chauffeur's uniform and carried his cap respectfully under his arm.

'Yes, I'm Miss Dawson.' Amanda's heart sank a little. She hadn't been told who would be meeting her and she had imagined it would probably be a secretary who would take her to her father's office. She would have lunch with her father, they would make each other's acquaintance and then he would return to his office and she would be free to browse round the London shops for the rest of the afternoon before she caught the train back to Exeter.

'I have a message for you, miss,' the chauffeur told her. 'Mr Dawson is sorry, but he has been unexpectedly delayed in Paris and he asks that I shall drive you to Radneys, to wait for him there. He thought it would be more comfortable for you than his London flat, which is unoccupied at present.'

'Radneys? Is it far?' She hoped sincerely that it wasn't. Even with a chauffeur to ferry her backwards and forwards to the station she might be pushed to catch a train early enough to link up with the last bus out to King's Holton.

The chauffeur gave her an odd look as if he were thinking that it was a funny daughter who didn't know where her father's house was. Perhaps he was new and didn't appreciate the circumstances. That made two of them, she decided rather glumly.

'Not very far, miss. If the traffic's not too bad on the motorway I can do it in an hour and a half.'

Amanda did a quick mental calculation. An hour and a half—that made three hours there and back. And her father had to come from Paris and then they had to have time to meet and talk and—— It just couldn't be done.

'Shall I take your luggage, miss?' The chauffeur was looking around for a non-existent case.

'I—I haven't brought any luggage,' she told him. 'You see, I hadn't planned to stay.'

The man grinned cheerfully. 'Oh well, not to worry, miss. Mrs French will see you have all you need, I'm sure. The car's parked over here, if you'll just follow me, miss. The name's Fogg, by the way.'

He turned and began to thread his way through the hurrying crowd of people, all intent upon getting somewhere or other as quickly as possible. Amanda hesitated a moment. This wasn't turning out at all as she had expected and the prospect of arriving at some grand house in the country without anything except what she carried in her handbag made her feel quite panicky. She glanced at Fogg's disappearing back and had a sudden urge to turn and make a bolt for it.

But that would be too childish for words, and anyway, she had promised. She must see this through now and get it over and done with as soon as possible. Then she could get back to Devon, to her friends and the way of life she was accustomed to and felt at home with.

The car, when they reached it, was huge and luxurious—a typical chauffeur-drive executive's car. Fogg opened the back door for her, but she looked inside at the capacious seats in fawn-coloured leather and pulled a face. 'I should be swallowed up all on my own there. I'll sit in front with you, if I may, Mr Fogg.' If she were really used to this kind of life she would have called him simply Fogg, she supposed. But she saw no reason to pretend a sophistication she didn't possess.

'Very pleased, I'm sure, miss,' beamed the chauffeur,

settling Amanda into the front passenger seat with the deference that might have been due to a princess. He got in behind the driving wheel and started the engine, which purred like a sleepy tiger. 'Sure you're comfortable, miss?'

'Yes, thank you,' said Amanda, smiling at him. This, she thought, is how the rich live. She had never before experienced such luxury and such cosseting and she wasn't sure that she really liked it.

She waited until the great silent car had woven its way through the thick traffic and out on to the motorway before she dared to speak to the driver again. Then she asked, 'How long have you been with my—with Mr Dawson?' She couldn't quite manage to say 'my father'.

'Oh, not very long, miss.' Fogg kept his eyes on the road. 'Me and the missus came to take up the position about six weeks ago. Very comfortable we are, too. Except for——' He stopped and then added firmly, 'Very comfortable.'

'Then you won't know about me?'

'About you, miss?'

'About the circumstances. You see, Mr Dawson is my father, but I've never really seen him before. His marriage to my mother broke up when I was a very small baby and my grandmother brought me up when my mother died, soon after. It was only last week that I heard from the solicitor that my father had decided he wanted to get to know me.'

Fogg forgot all about his deference. He let out an incredulous whistle as he slid a quick glance at the girl beside him, her wheat-fair hair framing a small, flower-like face with delicately pink cheeks. 'Blimey!' he said in broad Cockney. 'You're not arsking me to believe he's let a young lady like you slip all these years?'

Amanda grinned. 'I'm afraid so.'

'Then he wants his head examined,' was Fogg's disgusted reaction. He coughed, remembering himself. 'So what you're saying, miss, is that you're in a bit of a tricky situation.'

'I'm as nervous as a kitten,' she admitted, 'so if you could just—just fill in a few details of what to expect when I get to this house—Radneys, isn't it?—then I won't feel so strange. Just—well, who lives there, and so on.' She laughed in a strained way. 'It may sound absurd, but do you know I've no idea whether my father married again. I should have asked the solicitor, but I never thought of it. Is there a Mrs Dawson around?' Surely Mr Raikes would have told her if she had a stepmother. All the same, it was better to be prepared.

'No, miss, not that I know of. I've never heard of a Mrs Dawson.'

'Who lives in the house then, besides my father, and you and your wife, of course?'

'Well, there's Mrs French. She's there most of the time, and there's a good lot of visitors coming and going like. Parties, and so on.'

'Mrs French is the housekeeper?'

The chauffeur kept his eyes on the road. 'I suppose you could say that, miss.'

Amanda digested this scanty information. Fogg and his wife sounded ordinary enough. Most rich people seemed to rely on middle-aged couples to solve their staffing problems, she had heard. But who, exactly, was Mrs French? Her father's personal assistant—or secretary—or mistress? Well, it didn't matter to her, she assured herself, she'd only be staying one night anyway. But as the big car swallowed up the miles she began to feel more and more hollow inside at the prospect of what lay immediately ahead. It was just like the way she had imagined her father—to put her in this situation. Selfish, thoughtless, appearing so keen to know her and then not even bothering to be in the country to welcome her! What would this amiable chauffeur say if she told him she had changed her mind? If she said, 'I think, after all, it would be better if I came back another time, when my father is here.' Would he drive her back to London if she asked him?

His cheery voice broke in on her anxious doubts. 'Next junction, miss.' He began to edge the car across to the slow lane. 'Then it's only about five miles.'

Minutes later a transformation scene had come about. They had left the wide, busy roar of the motorway and were in deep country. Enormous trees formed tunnels over the road. The hedgerows were lush and green and the smell of growing things filled the air. 'Where are we, exactly?' Amanda enquired.

'South Gloucestershire, miss. Radneys is very convenient for the motorway. Mr Dawson has the best of both worlds, you might say—town and country.'

She was beginning to get the picture now. Mr Dawson, the important executive—Mr Dawson jetting round the Continent, unavoidably detained in Paris—Mr Dawson with his flat in London, his country house in Gloucestershire—Mr Dawson, casual, self-centred, indulging in a whim to see his unknown daughter. The more she saw the picture the less she liked it.

The car turned into a narrow lane with a high brick wall running along one side of it, and then into a winding drive, flanked by tall shrubs. At least the house would be beautiful; it must be, in these surroundings. An old manor house, probably, gracious and mellow and creeper-trimmed, with important chimneys and stone-mullioned windows; a house that had been built in the days when large families were fashionable and which still retained a warm feeling of nurseries, and strawberry blancmange, and hide-and-seek along shadowy passages. Gran had worked in a house like that when she was a girl and never tired of telling the young Amanda stories about it. Once they had been to glimpse the very house, peering across the parkland and through the trees. Amanda, then nine, had said, 'One day I shall marry a rich man and live in a house like that,' and Gran had laughed at her and said, 'You think a lot of yourself, don't you, young lady?'

She remembered that now, driving up to her father's house. Maybe he wasn't so bad after all; maybe he loved the countryside if he owned a beautiful old house right in the middle of this beautiful place. When she had read magazine articles claiming that the Cotswolds was the loveliest part of England she had always been ready to dispute that, considering Devon to hold that distinction, but now she was willing to admit that the Cotswolds might have a case.

The car pulled up and Fogg switched off the engine.

Amanda stared, then blinked. 'Is—is *this* the house?'

'Yes, miss, this is Radneys. Very modernistic, isn't it?'

'It certainly is,' said Amanda in a stunned voice.

The house bore no resemblance to the house of her imagination, except, perhaps, that a great deal of money had been spent upon the making of it. What she was looking at was a long, low, split-level, top-executive residence, dreamed up by an architect with a leaning towards the abstract and geometrical. Dazzling white cement, dark-stained timber slats, windows set at heights you wouldn't expect but no doubt made sense from the inside, wings emerging at right angles from the main building, and the whole covered by a flat green roof with projecting eaves supported by dark wooden cylinders—this was James Dawson's house in the country, as modern as the twenty-first century. Amanda gazed at it, torn between disappointment and a reluctant admiration. Her father had certainly won the glittering prizes, if that was what he wanted.

Inside the house Amanda followed the chauffeur into a living room the size of a swimming pool, with acres of pearl-grey carpet and a caterpillar settee in pale-green leather, smoky glass tables on supports of chromium tubes, tall leafy plants and aggressively modern pieces of sculpture. The room was on two levels and at the far end, up three wide steps, more green leather chairs were arranged to face the great sweep of glass overlooking smooth lawns with a wood in the distance.

'Sit down, won't you, miss,' said Fogg. 'I'll see if I can find Mrs French and tell her you're here.'

Amanda sat on the edge of one of the green leather chairs, which promptly swallowed her up. Just as if it had been a crocodile, she thought, trying to see the funny side of all this, though in truth she was wishing with all her heart that she was back in the shabby little house in King's Holton, and that her rich father hadn't suddenly remembered her existence. This luxurious, trendy place wasn't her scene and she felt like a fish out of water. Fish was good, she thought, suppressing a giggle, for the whole room was rather like some exotic underwater scene in a film. She half expected a man-eating shark to come gliding up, jaws snapping.

She was so intent on overcoming her jitters that she jumped when a woman's voice from behind her drawled, 'And so you're the schoolgirl daughter, are you?'

Amanda struggled out of the soft leather depths of the chair, to see a thin woman with orange-coloured hair regarding her out of eyes that looked as if they never had enough sleep. She wore a loose garment of black, thickly embroidered with gold dragons, which hung tiredly round her body—the kind of body that Gran would have called scrawny and said with a sniff that she didn't know why these middle-aged women had to diet themselves until they looked like barnyard hens.

'I'm Amanda Dawson,' said Amanda. 'I've come to see my father.'

The woman drifted round the end of the caterpillar settee and sank on to one of the cushions.

'Well, your father's not here.' She looked Amanda up and down without interest—well, she would hardly be interested in a grey flannel suit and a white silk blouse, would she? The outfit was new; Amanda had bought it as being suitable to look for a typing job in. When the summons came to meet her father in London she had debated whether to buy something less businesslike and had decided that as she didn't particularly want to impress her father, and as the money in her deposit account had been dwindling since Gran died, she would wear what she had. Now she was glad that she hadn't chosen to dress up for the occasion. Nothing that she might have chosen would have fitted into these lush surroundings. She stood within the semi-circle of chairs, being inspected by this unendearing woman and wondering if she should ask to be driven to the nearest station, and not wait to see her father after all. Only a certain dislike of giving up something she had started made her hesitate.

'Oh, for God's sake!' snapped the woman, who must be the Mrs French whose exact status in this house was as yet unexplained, although it was getting clearer every moment. 'Do you have to stand there like a gawk? You make me nervous. Make yourself useful, there's a good girl, and pour me a drink.' She jerked the orange-coloured head. 'Over there in the cabinet—the one at the end.'

Amanda hesitated for a moment and then complied. She didn't suppose Mrs French was being deliberately disagreeable. She probably treated everyone in this casual, rude way. But she couldn't help remembering how welcome Gran had made visitors, even ones she didn't much care for.

She opened the door of the built-in cabinet to disclose a miniature bar with shelves of bottles and glasses glittering under a strip-light.

'Vodka—with a small splash of lime.' The woman's voice was scratchy, like sandpaper.

Amanda stared at the bottles, found the ones that looked right and mixed the drink, guessing at the amounts. She carried it back to the woman on the settee, who downed it in a couple of gulps. 'God, I needed that!' She looked at

Amanda., 'Why aren't you drinking? Or don't nice little girls drink?' The hard mouth seemed set in a perpetual sneer.

Amanda regarded her levelly. 'It wouldn't be a very good idea, as I haven't eaten anything since half past six this morning.' It suddenly occurred to her that she was the daughter of the owner of this extravagant house, whatever the status of the woman with the orange hair. 'Perhaps I could have some lunch, if it's not too much trouble?'

The woman shot her a quick, suspicious look which Amanda met with her clear, grey-blue gaze. For fully ten seconds their eyes met and held, and it was Mrs French who looked away first. 'A healthy schoolgirl appetite!' She shuddered as if the idea were indecent. 'You'd better ring for Mrs Fogg, then—the cord over there.'

Almost immediately there was the faint brush of a door opening at the far end of the room and Amanda turned to see a woman advancing across the dove-grey carpet. She was small and neat in bottle-green, with wavy dark hair and a high colour. She gave Amanda a small smile that said, I know who you are, and Amanda smiled back. It was a relief to see someone in this house who reminded her of home and the people she knew there.

A bored voice from behind them said, 'This is Mr Dawson's darling daughter, Mrs F. She wants to eat, so you'd better take her away and feed her. Oh, and find her somewhere to sleep, will you. I suppose she'll have to stay the night as we don't know when Mr Dawson will be home. It'll have to be one of the side rooms, I'll need all the main ones for the people who want to stay on after the party.' A glint of orange hair showed above the back of the settee. 'What's your name, by the way? Do you call yourself Dawson?'

'Yes,' said Amanda. 'Amanda Dawson.'

'Amanda? How sweet and girlish! Come over here, Amanda.'

Amanda advanced to the back of the settee and stood looking down on slinky black glittering with gold dragons. Narrowed eyes stared at her with insolent appraisal. 'I suppose you'll have to come to my party tonight. Have you brought anything fit to wear?'

'No,' said Amanda, keeping her temper with an effort, 'I haven't brought anything at all. I didn't expect to come here or to have to stay overnight. And thank you for inviting me to your party, but I don't think I'll come.'

The yellowish eyes suddenly became vicious. 'Don't be a fool, girl, of course you'll come. What do you think your father would say to me if he got home and found you sulking in your room? Get along with Mrs Fogg now. I'll find something for you to wear later on.'

It wasn't worth arguing about at this stage, and anyway she was hungry. Never make decisions on an empty stomach, Gran had always said. But already she had decided that if there was no word of her father returning soon then she wouldn't stay on. She'd get back home if she had to walk all the way, rather than be subjected to any more of this woman's nastiness.

Mrs Fogg led the way over more acres of dove-grey carpet, round two corners. 'This is the bedroom wing, miss.' A long, long corridor with doors opening to left and right. Mrs Fogg opened a door at the very end. 'Perhaps you'll be comfortable here just for tonight, Miss Dawson. Tomorrow you could move into one of the larger rooms with its own shower—when Mrs French's guests have gone.' She sniffed, tossing her dark, neat head. She evidently had her own opinion of Mrs French's party guests.

'Oh, thank you, I'm sure I shall be quite comfortable. And I shan't be here tomorrow night.' Nor tonight, probably.

Mrs Fogg moved about the small, immaculate room, smoothing the quilted burgundy-red bedspread, flicking imaginary specks from the pale wood of the built-in dressing table, with its triple mirrors. 'It's a shame your father isn't here, miss, to welcome you.' Her eyes shone with knowing sympathy. She must have guessed accurately at the kind of welcome that Amanda had received from Mrs French. 'But you must ask me for anything you're wanting.' She adjusted the cord of the white venetian blind and sunlight poured into the room. 'The rooms on this side get the sun, but there's not much of a view. Now I'll see about some lunch for you, miss. Would you like it here or will you come to the dining room?'

'Oh, here, please, if it's not too much trouble,' Amanda said hastily. She didn't feel strong enough to brave this unfriendly house again yet.

'No trouble at all, miss. You just make yourself comfortable and I'll have something for you in a jiffy. The bathroom's next door.'

The bathroom was predictably elegant with fabulous toiletries on a built-out sill, a feathery plant in a matt white container, shrimp-pink ceramic ware and glassy black tiles. All so perfect that Amanda felt almost guilty about turning on the white onyx marble taps (they called them handwheels in the advertisements, didn't they?) But when she had swilled her face and hands she felt better. Back in the bedroom she walked to the window. She would have liked to pull up the venetian blind, but everything in this house inhibited her from action. Yes, she thought again, she would get away as soon as she could. The very thought of an evening party, among the friends of the horrid Mrs French, appalled her. If her father really wanted to see her, then fresh arrangements would have to be made for her to visit him in London.

Outside the window was a cemented area with shiny blue garage doors all along one side. She wondered how many cars her father kept. Fogg was busy polishing the black limousine they had driven in from London, whistling cheerily. He was nice, Amanda decided, and his wife too.

If she asked them, surely they would help her to get away.

She sat down by the window and began to leaf through the copy of *Vogue* she had brought with her. The women's clothes didn't seem nearly so way-out seen in these lush surroundings. The girl in the sleek, off-the-shoulder item in coppery lace with a thigh-high slit up the front would look just right in that ultra-modern living room with the pale green leather chairs.

And here was the man in the background again, standing behind her. He was half in shadow and that gave him a mysterious, disturbing quality. The girl was turned away from him, her head thrown back in laughter and he was smiling slightly, aware that he had said something amusing; faintly deprecating, yet very, very sure of himself and his impact. His hand on her bare shoulder seemed just to have been placed there and his head was leaning towards her. He really was stunningly attractive: dark hair flicking back above his ear, a hint of a lean muscular body, a flash of white teeth against deeply tanned skin, eyes squeezed up in a smile.

Amanda sighed and wondered again if there really were men like that or if they lived only between the covers of magazines, expertly made up and posed by a skilful photographer. Certainly she had never met one. She remembered the first time she had gone out on a date with a boy, a young farmer from the neighbouring village, and Gran's anxious advice: 'Don't forget, dear, men only want one thing. You need to take care—a young girl gets carried away so quickly.'

Dear Gran—it couldn't be easy for an elderly woman to bring up a girl in these permissive days. But her advice hadn't really been needed. It hadn't been in the least difficult to fend off the inexpert fumblings that accompanied the goodnight kiss outside the cottage door and she had never, in later dates with that boy and one or two others, found herself in the slightest danger of getting 'carried away'.

She sighed now, looking at the photograph, wondering just what it was that gave this man a quality that set up a faint disturbance inside her. Would she ever meet a man like that who would carry her away into dizzy realms of delight and desire, or was that merely a fantasy of all eighteen-year-olds?

She came back to earth as Mrs Fogg came in, carrying a tray. 'I'll put it here on the small table for you, miss. Steak and mushrooms.' She lifted the casserole dish lid, letting out a savoury smell. 'There's creme caramel here and coffee in the flask.'

'Oh, thank you, Mrs Fogg, it smells delicious.'

'It's a pleasure, miss, I'm sure, to have someone who enjoys her food. Mrs French, now, never eats lunch and only picks at her dinner.' She turned to the door. 'Is there anything else, Miss Dawson?'

Amanda seized her chance. 'Well, I was just wondering if—if I wanted to leave soon whether Mr Fogg would be able to take me to the nearest main line station?'

'You won't be waiting to see your father, then, miss?' The woman looked quite disappointed.

'I haven't quite made up my mind yet, but I think perhaps I ought to get back home to—to see to things there,' Amanda improvised.

Mrs Fogg folded her arms and stood looking at her, lips pursed. 'Yes, miss, I quite understand,' she said, and from her expression Amanda thought that probably she did. 'I'll ask my husband if you like and then I can let you know later.'

'Thank you very much.' Amanda smiled her gratitude and when Mrs Fogg had departed she propped the copy of *Vogue* against the dressing table mirror and applied herself to her lunch.

She had just finished her coffee when the sound of a car

drawing up outside the window made her peer between the slats of the venetian blind to see a silver-grey, low-slung monster slide to a halt. A tall man got out and slammed the door, standing with his back to her. Her father? No, he looked too young to be her father. Even from the back his body looked lithe and strong and his hair was dark, with the sheen of perfect health.

Fogg stopped polishing and looked up with a grin. 'Afternoon, Mr Craddock.'

'Hullo, Fogg, how's life? Mr Dawson back from Paris yet?'

The voice came clearly through the window. It was deep and resonant. A confident voice. Oddly, something inside Amanda vibrated in response.

'Not yet, sir, there's some sort of hold-up. I'm waiting for a call now to meet him at the airport. Leave your car, sir, I'll put her in for you. That's if you're staying overnight?'

The man nodded. 'Yes, I am. Thanks, Fogg.'

He turned round then and she saw his face and her eyes opened wide in amazement. 'I don't believe it,' she said out loud. She looked at the *Vogue* photograph and then back to the man outside. The likeness was uncanny. The man seemed to have stepped out of the photograph straight into her life.

Then she saw the difference. This man was older—in his thirties, probably. The magazine man was just posing as a Top Person while the driver of the sleek grey car was the real thing. It was the way her mind had been working that had provided the shock of recognition, that and the general look of the man: the way his dark hair grew, the wide, somehow exciting curve of his mouth, the narrowed dark-lashed eyes that seemed to smile.

She watched him until he disappeared inside the opposite wing of the house, by a side door next to the garages. Then she started as she saw that Mrs Fogg had come into the room without her hearing. 'Did you enjoy your lunch, miss?' the housekeeper enquired.

Amanda blinked herself back to sanity. 'Oh—oh yes, very much thank you, it was lovely.'

'That's right, then. I'll take the tray. Oh, and I had a word with Dave—that's my husband—and he says he's sorry he must be here on call to meet your father, but if you really have to get to Bristol he could——'

Amanda said quickly, 'No, please don't bother him, Mrs Fogg. It was just a thought—it isn't all that urgent.'

'Well, if you're sure, miss?'

'Yes, quite sure, thank you.'

She was staying overnight. The man who had just driven up in the grey car was staying overnight, so she would almost be sure to meet him. It might be amusing to find out what he was like at closer quarters. Probably, she assured herself, she would be completely disillusioned.

But her heart insisted on beating a little faster at the prospect.

CHAPTER TWO

AMANDA slipped the cerise satin dress over her head, smoothed it on the hips and stood back looking doubtfully at her reflection in the bedroom.

'Don't you think—isn't it a bit *old* for me?' she said, unconsciously using the word Gran would have used.

'Old?' Mrs French, lounging back on the bed, still wearing the black caftan with the gold dragons, yawned and said, 'My dear, don't be tedious, you can't wear schoolgirl clothes for the rest of your life. It fits you very well, and anyway it's the only one I've got in your size—I take a small twelve myself now.' She gazed down complacently at the skinny form beneath the caftan.

Amanda looked back to the mirror. She didn't want to be ungrateful and Mrs French did seem to be doing her best to be amiable now. Also, she had heard from Mrs Fogg that Mrs French had spent the afternoon in bed with a migraine, and she could sympathise with that. Gran had suffered from headaches and Amanda knew what havoc they could play with a normally pleasant disposition. Not that she had seen much sign of pleasantness about Mrs French up to now, but at least she had gone to the trouble of looking out a dress for Amanda to wear at the party.

But what a dress! In her wildest schoolgirl dreams of sophistication she had never imagined herself wearing anything like this. There was hardly any top at all and the neckline plunged to the waist, disclosing almost as much as it concealed of her firm young breasts. A close-fitting pointed hip yoke ended low in a silver tassel, and smaller tassels brushed her upper arms, hanging from the shoulders in the slits of short wing sleeves. The long skirt was composed of panels front and back, with slits either side reaching high up the thighs. It was an expensive, elegant, provocative dress, and Amanda suffered qualms of apprehension as she pictured herself walking into a room in it. But there was an odd sense of excitement as well.

'But—but my bra shows,' she murmured.

Mrs French burst into a loud laugh. 'Then take it off. You won't need your village maiden modesty here, you know.' She slid lazily off the bed. 'Well, there you are, it's the best I can do for you. There's a nightdress there and a wrap'—she indicated some wisps of chiffon on the bed —'and you'll find make-up in a box in the closet. Anything else you'll need is in the bathroom next door. Now I suppose I'd better go and dress myself before the crowd descends upon us.' She tossed back the dregs of the drink she had brought in with her. 'God, my head's still absolutely foul, I don't know how I'm going to get through tonight.'

And without another look at Amanda she drifted languidly out of the room.

Amanda turned back to the mirror, still doubtful. Then a small, fighting glint came into her eyes. She had chosen to stay, hadn't she? She had agreed to go to this party tonight. This was her father's world. She didn't think she was going to like it one bit, but it was only fair to take a long calm look at it before she made up her mind. Remembering what she had heard and read about the 'swinging' parties of the very rich, she felt a slight sinking at the pit of her stomach, but she told herself she didn't have to join in anything she didn't want to, and she was quite capable of looking after herself. It was going to be a challenge, and Amanda had never shirked a challenge. Also there was the prospect of seeing the man-in-the-background again—if only from the distance—and that might be fun.

With a small smile playing round her pretty mouth she slipped out of the cerise dress, hung it carefully on its hanger, and, putting on the filmy black wrap from the bed, she made for the bathroom.

An hour later she was almost ready. She had enjoyed wallowing in scented water in the shrimp-pink bath and speculating frivolously and with inward giggles about the man who was so like the fabulous man-in-the-background of the *Vogue* photograph. What made these photograph men so intriguing, she decided, was that you never quite knew what their relationship was to the model girl. There they were, brooding darkly, and you couldn't decide if they were husband, boy-friend, lover; if they had known each other for ages or had just met. Or even if they hadn't met at all but wanted to. She was still pondering the subject as she slid into the sophisticated and revealing cerise dress and put on a make-up a little heavier than the one she usually wore.

As she finished putting a final burnish on her silky mink-fair hair and arranging it softly round her face, the door opened and Mrs French appeared again. At the sight of her Amanda suppressed a smile, thinking that she needn't have bothered about her own appearance being *outré* while this woman was around. Mrs French was wearing a skin-tight dress of spring green crêpe, heavily encrusted with gold sequins, and her orange hair was brushed into a spiky urchin style which would have looked piquante on a young girl but had the effect of making the woman look like a thin, haggard clown. Earrings and bracelets swung and clinked as she moved and her hands were heavy with rings, the stones in which were of such a size that Amanda wondered if they could possibly be real.

She came further into the room, bringing with her a drift of musky perfume. 'Aren't you ready yet? They're nearly all here and I shan't have much time to devote to you—you'd better come along now.' She looked Amanda over critically. 'H'm—not too bad! But you haven't much idea of make-up, have you? Here, let me.' She picked up the eye-brush from the dressing table and pushed Amanda on to the stool, plying the brush with sharp strokes. 'And that lipstick's quite wrong—much too pale with that dress. Wipe it off.'

Amanda took the tissue held out to her and, for a moment, struggled with a strong temptation to throw it in the woman's face and walk out. Then she seemed to hear Gran's voice saying, 'In for a penny, in for a pound,' and did as she was told. She had made up her mind to treat this party as an experience, a quick glimpse into another world, and she had to conform to its particular fashions if she didn't want to appear conspicuous, which she certainly didn't.

She wiped off the pink lipstick and applied the burgundy red one that Mrs French selected. Surveying her image in the mirror she thought wryly, I look like a tart—is that what she wants?

'That's better,' approved Mrs French. 'But your hair's too little-girl for words.' She took the brush and swept Amanda's silky hair away from one ear and across the back of her head, letting it fall into a heavy, pale mass on her right shoulder.

'That's all I've got time for now.' Mrs French's smile was more like a grimace. 'We can't have you looking like a milkmaid, can we? I shan't introduce you as James Dawson's daughter, that'd need too many explanations, and anyway I'm sure James would prefer to meet you first himself. You can just come along as my friend, nobody will ask questions. I'll just call you Amanda and you'd better call me Elaine. Understood?'

Amanda nodded. Her stomach felt rather odd again, but she was going through with this, come what might. 'Have you heard when my father is expected home yet?'

'He's on his way—Fogg has gone off to Heathrow to meet him. He should be here some time later tonight.' At the door the orange-coloured head turned sharply. 'Come along, what are you waiting for?'

Amanda met the woman's impatience with her clear gaze. 'I just thought—if I'm to meet your friends, don't you think I should have some idea of—of what your own position is here?'

Elaine French's mouth hardened. 'Oh, you want to have everything nice and straight, do you?' Her tone was almost venomous and the look she threw at Amanda was one of pure dislike. Then she seemed to think better of it and said more calmly, 'Well, briefly, your father is my brother-in-law. His wife, my sister, killed herself in a car crash a year ago. Since then I've stayed on and looked after things here for your father, as he goes abroad a good deal. I imagine that your father and I will come to some—er—arrangement fairly soon. That satisfy you?'

'You mean you're going to get married?'

'Clever girl, aren't you?' Elaine French sneered.

Amanda bit her lip. That settled it, she decided, as she followed the woman out of the room and down the long carpeted corridor. This was going to be a short—a very short—visit, whatever her father wanted.

The huge living room looked very different from the last time Amanda had seen it. The caterpillar of pale green leather had been split up into casual units and arranged round the sides. Concealed lighting threw a dull pearl glow over the whole room, falling silkily on the bare arms and shoulders of the women and the fashionable evening clothes of the men. As Amanda followed Elaine French through the haze of smoke, between the groups of guests, she was thankful that she was dressed and made up so that she wouldn't look conspicuous among this sophisticated throng of people. If she had to come to a party like this it was far more comfortable to be able to merge into the background.

The room was crowded. The smell of cigar smoke drifted on the motionless air, mingling with French perfume and the scent of hothouse flowers. Below the chatter the velvety throb of beat music came from some unseen source.

Elaine French made her way across the crowded room, greeting everyone with a kind of feverish gaiety. All the women looked about Elaine's own age, and seemed to Amanda to breathe an air of expensive dress shops and beauty salons. The men looked prosperous—executives who ate and drank on generous expense accounts, close-shaved, mottle-faced with puffy eyelids over slightly bleared eyes. Amanda shivered inside. Was her father like this? she wondered bleakly. Was this what Gran had meant when she said, 'Your father isn't a good man'? She wasn't prepared to judge whether these people were 'good', in Gran's meaning of the word, or not. She only knew that she felt out of her element and out of her depth among them.

The bar at the raised end of the room glittered in contrast to the muted lighting in the rest of the room. Here Elaine stopped and put a hand on the arm of one of the men pouring drinks. 'Laurie, this is Amanda. Be a sweetie and get her a drink, will you?' She kept her hand on his arm and the look that passed between them seemed to Amanda to hold a message of some sort. Confusedly she wondered whether Elaine and this man were specially intimate. That was how it seemed, but perhaps she was imagining things. In an atmosphere like this one could imagine almost anything.

Elaine turned back to her. 'You'll be all right now, dear. Laurie will look after you,' she cooed, and moved away from them.

Amanda stared after her, amazed. *Dear?* And that sugary tone of voice? What did it mean?

'Well now, this *is* cosy.' The man's voice, close to her ear, was slurred and his breath informed her unpleasantly that he had been drinking for some considerable time. 'What's it to be?'

She spun round, finding his face much too close to her own, and drew away quickly. 'What's *what* to be?'

'What do you think?' He smiled foolishly. 'Drinkie, of course.'

Amanda looked at him with distaste. He was tall and lanky, a little younger than most of the other men around, but already growing paunchy. With tow-coloured hair and a moustache that drooped over a red, moist mouth, he had a disagreeably foxy look.

'I——' she began. She almost asked for a tomato juice, but then she thought that she must go on acting in the character she had assumed, now that she had started. To admit that she was a country girl who had witnessed this kind of party only on TV would be extremely humiliating at this stage, although she was beginning to glimpse a possibility that it might come to that in the end. 'I leave it to you,' she murmured.

His hot brown eyes slid over her in a way she didn't care for at all. 'That's what I like to hear a girl say.' He turned back to the bar and Amanda looked round desperately for possible escape, but there was no way through the groups of people clustered thickly between her and the door at the far end of the long room.

The man was back then, holding two drinks unsteadily in one hand. The other hand, hot on her waist through the thin stuff of her dress, urged her towards a dim corner of the room. 'Now we can get to know each other—Amanda.' He put the drinks down and drew her beside him on to one of the leather settees that had been arranged to accommodate two. She felt his hand on her waist again, his moist warm fingers moving lower to probe the soft rounded flesh of her thigh where the slit skirt fell apart. She moved away, but he pulled her back. 'Relax, sweetheart, and drink up.' He raised one of the glasses to her lips and then drank from it himself.

'Here's to all your—er—charms,' he murmured, his eyes on the cleavage of the cerise dress.

He put her drink into her hand and then finished off his own. 'You're not madly keen to play tonight, are you, sweetheart? We could easily find something more—interesting—to fill the time.' His voice was thick with innuendo, his mouth against her cheek, his breath coming unevenly.

'Play?' Amanda gazed wildly round the room. Somehow she must escape, and quickly.

Then she saw what he had referred to. The guests were all moving towards the centre of the room, where a circle of hanging shaded lights had been switched on, illuminating something she hadn't noticed before, a large, baize-covered table on which stood the trappings of some gambling game—roulette, or some such. There was a wheel and a large squared board and stacks of counters.

'I think I would like——' she began, and got to her feet. She had no money with her, and not much in her handbag in the bedroom, but anything was better than remaining with this odious Laurie individual.

Then, like an answer to prayer, the crowds round the bar began to drift away to the gaming table and she saw him standing there—the man-in-the-background. Just as she had imagined him, urbane, self-contained and fabulously good-looking in his dark jacket, leaning back against the side of the bar panelling, glass held nonchalantly in hand.

The sight of him did something very strange to Amanda's breathing. It was very odd, this feeling that it had happened before, and so it had, of course, in her imagination. All afternoon, when she had gone out to explore the small village, to watch the ducks on the pond, to wander round the great Cotswold 'wool' church, she had played a romantic, foolish game with herself about this man. Once, while she was examining the carving on the lectern, she heard heavy footsteps approaching her and turned, her heart thumping, half expecting to see him walking up the aisle. But it was only a large lady with a brush and dustpan, and when she had passed with a pleasant 'Good afternoon', Amanda had laughed at herself for being such an idiot.

But now the man had come straight out of her dream and he was looking across the room at her, and he didn't seem like a stranger at all. Quite involuntarily, as she met his steady glance, she smiled at him, tilting her head a little, her mass of mink-fair hair caressing one white shoulder.

It wasn't exactly a smile that he sent back in return, but she saw the glint in his dark eyes and a slight pull of the muscles beside his mouth. Then, quite slowly, he detached himself from the bar panelling and sauntered across the room to them.

'Hullo, sweetheart.' He put an arm lightly round her shoulder. 'It's been a long, long time. Nobody told me you were here. Where have you been hiding all these months?'

Laurie was on his feet now, swaying slightly, tipsily aggressive. 'Hey, what's all this? Amanda's with me and you can take yourself off, Blair.'

The newcomer surveyed him with tolerant amusement. 'Ah no, you've got it wrong, laddie. It's you who takes yourself off. Exit Laurie, this is your cue.'

'But Elaine said——' The flushed face was stupidly puzzled.

'Yes, I know, I know,' the dark man soothed. 'But Elaine says all sorts of zany things, you should know that. Amanda and I are old friends, we've got a lot to talk about, haven't we, sweetheart?' He gave her shoulder a squeeze, firm fingers sinking gently into her flesh, which to her confusion sent ripples of pleasure down her spine.

She looked up doubtfully to meet dark, amused eyes. 'Y-yes, of course.'

He turned back to Laurie. 'There you are, old man. Satisfied?'

'No, I'm not satisfied!' Laurie was becoming belligerent. 'She's my girl.'

'Oh no, she's not your girl—never for one second is she your girl.' Amanda caught the note of hard contempt behind the smooth voice. 'Go along, Laurie, take yourself off.'

Laurie lurched towards the other man, thrusting out a nondescript chin, his fair moustache drooping damply.

'You think a bloody sight too much of yourself, Mr Blair Craddock. I'll be damned if I'll go.'

The dark man smiled for the first time and there was danger in his smile. Amanda felt a tremor of fear—there wasn't going to be a fight, was there?

But she needn't have worried. He merely stretched out and gathered the frills of Laurie's pink evening shirt in one one hand, giving a slight backward push. Laurie, none too steady on his feet to start with, collapsed into the enveloping depths of the settee behind him. He made an ineffective attempt to get up but sank back again.

'Finish your drink,' said the dark man. He pushed a glass into Laurie's unsteady hand. 'Be seeing you, chum.'

Then he moved aside the long velvet curtains that covered the patio window, which was standing partly open. 'Come along, Amanda, I need some fresh air.'

He held the curtain for her and she stepped out on to the paved terrace. After the hot, smoke-hazy room it was good to feel the cool evening air on her cheeks. They walked together down a flight of shallow steps to the lawn. 'Let's go and take a look at the river first, shall we?' he said, and linked his arm through hers.

First? Was he going to take her on a tour of the estate, then? That would suit her fine—to get away from that awful party and be out here in the cool darkness with this intriguing man who had suddenly stepped out of the background into the centre of her world. How extraordinary—unbelievable, really—the way it had all happened. And now she was walking here with Blair, conscious of the smooth cloth of his coat sleeve against her arm. Blair—the name was right for him, for his dark relaxed good looks, his deep, lazily arrogant voice, his sleepy eyes that had suddenly flamed into anger a few moments ago. Dreamily Amanda found herself leaning towards him as they walked over the grass, with the smell of a summer garden in the air and the soft turf sucking at the pencil-thin high heels of Elaine's silver evening shoes.

His hold on her arm tightened and he rubbed his cheek against the top of her head. 'This is a bonus,' he said softly. 'One doesn't expect to find anything like you at one of Elaine's parties.'

'I could say the same about you,' she said, and laughed. It was quite extraordinary how easy she felt with him—not a bit shy, although he was a stranger and so much older than any of the young men she had known.

'A couple of misfits, that's what we are. We must console each other, don't you agree?' he said gravely.

He led her through a gap in the high laurel hedge that bordered the lawn and along a wide path overhung by silver birch saplings, their delicate branches glimmering in the moonlight.

'It's lovely here,' Amanda sighed. 'Like fairyland.'

'Do you see yourself as the fairy queen? You're lovely enough, Amanda.'

She gave a little gurgle of laughter. 'Hardly, in this get-up.' She glanced down at the showy cerise dress. He was fooling, of course, but something in his voice sent a ripple of excitement coursing through her body. He was surely a little taken by her—he must be or he wouldn't have bothered to take her away from that odious Laurie person.

She said, 'I didn't thank you for rescuing me, just now. It was positively masterly, pretending to know me.'

She saw the gleam of white teeth against tanned skin, thick dark lashes that swept his cheek, intriguing little curved lines that bracketed the long, straight mouth. His smile was as exciting as everything else about him.

'I thought that you rated something better than Laurie Fellowes and that you weren't enjoying yourself very much. Was I right?'

'I was hating every minute of it.'

'And I calculated that my intervention would be welcome?'

'Oh, indeed it was,' she breathed.

'Good,' he said. He sounded pleased, satisfied. 'I

shouldn't like there to be any misunderstanding. It seems we feel the same way about each other.'

Her heart jolted at his words. Was he telling her in his own way that he had fallen in love with her in that first moment their eyes met? The words of the old song came into her mind: 'Some enchanted evening—you may see a stranger—you may see a stranger across a crowded room——' She swallowed quickly. These words, that swooning melody, had always had the power to make her knees feel weak and her throat close up.

They had reached the river now, a silver snake in the moonlight, with mysterious shadows under the overhanging bushes, and stood side by side looking down where the water moved slowly, gurgling faintly over its stones.

'Lovely,' said Amanda.

'Lovely,' echoed Blair Craddock. His arm detached itself from hers and slipped round her shoulders, his fingers fastening on the little silver tassel that swung against her arm. 'You, I mean, of course.'

She heard him catch his breath and then felt his lips against her neck, cool and hard in the hollow where the neckline of her dress plunged downwards. 'Lovely,' he whispered again, and turned her towards him.

His face was dark and shadowy above hers as he held her away, looking down at her, his fingers touching her neck, her temple, her cheek and coming to rest on her mouth. It was very still and very quiet—a velvet evening with only the faint gurgle of the water and the threadlike chirrup of crickets. Amanda shivered, waiting on the brink of ecstasy.

Then, with a small sigh, his mouth took hers.

It was like no kiss she had ever had before. It was gentle, seeking, somehow questioning, and as his lips moved against hers every nerve and fibre of her body responded by an instinct that had never been aroused before. Her lips parted sweetly as his kiss became deeper, more demanding. Her arms went round his neck and her fingers buried themselves in the thick dark hair there. She didn't think what might happen next, she was beyond thought, lost in the wonder of the moment, the joy of first love that was so much happiness that it was almost sadness.

When he took his mouth from hers she could have wept. 'I think,' he said, 'we'd better go in.'

She felt a twinge of fear. 'Not—not back to that party?'

His arm went round her waist comfortably as they started to walk back along the path under the silver birches. 'What do *you* think?' he said.

He took her into the house through a door in one of the side wings and up a short flight of slatted stairs, at the top of which was a door leading into what seemed to be a private apartment, separate from the rest of the house. Separate—and different. The room was furnished comfortably; brown linen covers on the easy chairs, bookcases, bulging with books, which overflowed on to the floor and every available horizontal surface, a big writing desk where (in contrast to the books) neatness and order appeared to prevail. There were lots of pictures on the walls, modern but not perplexingly so, and several pieces of furniture which looked Oriental. Concealed lights threw a soft glow over the whole room.

'Sit down,' said Blair, nodding towards a settee, 'and I'll get us something to drink.' He went to a cupboard in the corner and came back holding two glasses filled with an amber liquid. 'Try that,' he said. 'It's a special of my own, that's why I didn't ask you what you'd have. Every new visitor here has to try it, I make it a rule.' He smiled over the rim of his glass. 'To our meeting, Amanda.'

Shyly, she murmured, 'Our meeting,' and sipped the drink. It was pleasant—cool and fruity and it didn't taste very strong, for which she was thankful. She didn't want to feel even slightly hazy—she wanted to savour every second of this time with him. She said, 'These are your own rooms, then?'

He nodded, sitting down on the settee beside her. 'A business arrangement,' he explained rather vaguely.

Oh, but that was marvellous! He must be a close associate of her father's, so perhaps she would be able to see him again, quite often. Not that she was going to live here, of course, she had already decided against that, even supposing her father wanted her to. But she could come and visit him some time and——

His hand covered hers and slid up her arm to the dangling silver tassel. 'Snappy!' he said, and grinned, swinging the tassel from side to side.

She grinned back. She felt at ease here—at home. She slipped her feet out of the high-heeled silver shoes. 'Ah, that's better!' she sighed. She wouldn't tell him they were Elaine's shoes, and that it was Elaine's dress she was wearing—not yet. She would have to tell him soon, and about being James's daughter, but for the moment explanations could wait. They would take too long and waste too much precious time. As she sipped her drink she thought, Soon he'll kiss me again, and she felt weak and shaken at the thought.

She looked at the hand holding the glass—a strong man's hand, but fine-skinned for all its sinewy power, brown and long-fingered, the nails immaculate. His other hand was still playing with the silver tassel at her neck and she trembled inside every time his fingers brushed her arm.

His legs were stretched out in front of him and now he gently kicked at the silver shoes she had discarded. 'Good idea,' he said. 'I'll follow suit,' and he put down his glass, leaned forward and unlaced his own shoes, placing them beside the silver ones. 'Go well together,' he mused softly. 'But I still think you have the advantage of me.'

She glanced at him uncertainly and then saw what he

meant as he pulled off his tie and tossed it aside, unbutton-
ing the top buttons of his shirt. Unlike the other men at
the party, he was not wearing evening dress, but a dark
lightweight suit with a white shirt. Now the shirt fell open
at the neck, disclosing a sunburned chest with a tangle of
wiry dark hair. 'That's better.' He lay back on the settee,
drawing her against him until her head lay on his shoulder. 'Nice,' he murmured. 'Comfy?'

Amanda sighed, her cheek against the fine stuff of his
shirt. She could feel the warmth of his body through it, the
steady strong beat of his heart. He was wonderful, she
thought dreamily, not like the boys at home in the village;
she smothered a chuckle thinking that by now, in a situation like this, she would have to be fighting them off. But
not this man—not Blair. He had—what was it?—a civilised, adult approach. He wasn't the callow kind like Laurie
either.

'Finish your drink,' he said. He picked it up and put it
into her hand, and she tried to drink it without moving
away from him, which was almost impossible.

She choked, wriggled, and her dress slipped off one shoulder, exposing a pink taut young breast, innocent of any con-
straining bra. She grabbed the dress and hitched it back
again hastily.

'Must you?' Blair's voice was lazy, amused. 'You looked
so nice as you were.'

She glanced up at him uncertainly, but his eyes were
twinkling with conscious wickedness, inviting her to see the
joke. 'If the dress is bothering you why not take it off?' he
suggested, and as she suddenly shot upright he added
suavely, 'There's a blue silk thing hanging in the bathroom
if you really must cover up your charms.' He was laughing
at her now.

She relaxed with a small grin. 'Thanks, I'll do that,' she
said, and got to her feet.

He stood up too and took her empty glass and put it on

the low table in front of them. 'Another?' he asked. 'To make up for what you've spilt?'

'No, thanks.' She glanced round hastily, looking for the bathroom. There was something in his eyes as he looked down at her, in the too-revealing dress, that made her heart race. Somewhere at the very back of her mind was a niggling thought that she shouldn't stay here, alone in what was evidently a man's private apartment, but she pushed it away quickly. She couldn't leave now—she might never have a chance to be alone with him again for ages and ages. And they had only just begun to get to know each other. She wanted to talk to him, to find out about him. She would tell him who she was and he would tell her about her father and about their work together. And—and—her mind emptied itself of all the sensible, practical things—and more than anything she wanted him to kiss her again.

In the small, compact bathroom she found the blue wrapper, and, slipping off her dress, slid into its cool, pure silk folds. She was sure it was pure silk—although she had never worn anything of pure silk before—and of a heavenly deep blue. It wasn't very much too large for her; it must, she thought, be a short style with elbow-length sleeves to fit Blair. She tied the girdle round her waist and turned to the mirror, a secret little smile curving her mouth. 'You're an abandoned woman,' she told herself silently, 'and I'm ashamed of you—undressing in a man's bathroom!'

For a turbulent moment she wondered what it would be like if it were true—if she had really come here to—to—— Her imagination caught fire and went up in a spiral of flame, and suddenly, once again, she remembered Gran's words, 'Young girls get so easily carried away.' Suddenly she felt very naïve and ignorant. In spite of the books she had read, the magazine articles, the TV plays she had watched, the rather giggle-inspiring instruction at school, she knew she was stupidly inexperienced.

But Blair wouldn't go too far, she felt sure of that. He

had a kind of sensitivity and he wasn't a casual womaniser. He couldn't be, could he? Look how he had suggested that she should take off that sexy dress and put on something that covered her up!

And something had happened between them in that first moment. She knew that he had recognised it, just as she had herself. Something shattering. He wouldn't want to spoil it by a too hasty expression of a love that was going to grow and grow.

Amanda had often wondered what it would be like to fall in love. Now she knew. It was like an earthquake.

When she went back into the living room Blair was pouring himself another drink. 'Sure you won't have one?' he asked over his shoulder.

She stood in the middle of the room, the cerise dress hanging limply over her arm. 'N-no, thank you,' she faltered. She couldn't take her eyes off him. How elegant he was, with his long legs and narrow hips, his shoulders wide under the pale, silky shirt, his thick dark hair rumpled at the back where her fingers had buried themselves in it down by the river. She shivered as she remembered.

He turned round, his eyes moving over her lazily in the thin blue gown, and a curious look flashed across his face and was gone again. 'Very becoming,' he said, 'what are you going to do with *that*?' He nodded towards her arm.

She looked down vaguely at the cerise dress. 'Oh, I'll put it somewhere——' She moved to throw it over the back of a chair, but he said quickly, 'You'd better hang it up. It would be a pity to let it get crushed, wouldn't it? Such a fancy little number as it is!'

She glanced at him doubtfully and saw the glint in his dark eyes. That was a confusing, intriguing thing about the man. You didn't quite know whether he was serious or not.

'You'll find a hook behind the door in there,' he said, nodding towards a communicating door which stood half open. The room beyond was in darkness, but there was suf-

ficient light seeping through for Amanda to see that it was
a bedroom. Her limbs felt suddenly heavy; it was quite an
effort to make her legs take her through the open doorway
into the dim room. She could just make out the shape of
a low, large bed in the middle of the room. With frenzied
haste she groped behind the door, found a padded hanger
there and thrust the dress on to it. She was reaching up to
put it back on the hook when she was aware that Blair had
come silently into the room and was standing close behind
her. She stood frozen, arms raised, holding her breath, and
her heart thumped in great heavy beats. The hanger
dropped from her fingers and the dress slithered silently to
the floor.

'Tut-tut,' murmured Blair, and he stooped and picked it
up. Without looking round she sensed that he was smoothing the dress on the hanger. He reached round her and
hung it up. 'There,' he said, giving it a little pat. Then his
hand came down and rested on Amanda's waist, the other
hand joined it on the opposite side, and very slowly he
turned her round to face him. 'Don't you think,' he said
softly, 'that we've wasted enough time?'

She had never wanted anything in her life so over-
poweringly as she wanted his kiss. She tipped back her
head and closed her eyes. Yes,' she murmured. 'Oh, yes.'

His mouth came down on hers as her lips parted, and
his kiss was practised, arousing, devastatingly sensual. Her
senses swam as his hands loosened the sash of the blue
gown and slid beneath it, caressing the soft smoothness of
her back, her waist, moving her a little away so that he
could cup the swelling roundness of her breasts. 'Lovely,'
he murmured against her lips. 'You're lovely.' Then she
was being lifted in his arms as if she had no weight at all,
and she found herself lying on the bed. He was beside her
and his body was silhouetted against the light that came
through the doorway from the living room. He was pulling
off his shirt. 'Too many clothes between us,' he murmured,

and she saw his hand go to the belt of his trousers. Then he paused, leaning over her, resting on his hands. 'This is what you want too, isn't it, sweetheart? This is why you invited me?'

Invited! The word struck her as if he had thrown a bucket of icy water full in her face. Her reeling senses steadied; her body was numb and chilled. With a tremendous effort she pushed him away and sat up, dragging the silk robe round her. 'I didn't invite you, you know I didn't!'

She sensed rather than saw his unbelieving smile. 'Is this a new line you're trying out, because I'm not sure I like it. You didn't invite me, didn't you? Well, you can remedy that straight away.'

His arms went round her again, forcing her down on the bed as he swung his body over hers, and this time there was no gentleness. He was all masculine aggression, hard, seeking.

'No. *No!*' Amanda forced out between clenched teeth. 'Stop—I mean it, please stop. I didn't—I swear I didn't——' She pushed at him with all her strength, her whole body tense and rigid. Somewhere at the back of her mind she knew she had been wrong, crazy, to come here, but she hadn't known—— The whole thing had gone wrong. It was cheap—degrading—and somehow it was her fault. Sobs choked her as she went on struggling. Then suddenly she was aware that his arms were no longer holding her and light dazzled her eyes as he switched on the bedside lamp. He was standing by the bed looking down at her as she lay there shivering and his face was cold with anger.

'You little——' he began, and stopped. 'There are plenty of words for girls like you. No doubt you're familiar with all of them if you indulge often in this sort of amusement.' His lip curled. 'And what about the men who *don't* object to taking an unwilling girl? How do you deal with them? Do you conceal a small stiletto around your person, perhaps? Or a dainty little gun?' He went over and took the cerise dress off the hanger and tossed it over to her. 'Though I should have thought,' he gave her dishevelled figure an insolent stare, 'that you'd have some difficulty in finding a place to conceal *anything* in that dress. You'd better put it on again and then get the hell out of here, back to your sleazy party.'

Somehow she sat up on the bed, grabbing the silk wrap round her. 'Oh, please—please! I don't know what you mean—truly I don't. I thought——' Her mouth shook as she remembered just what she *had* thought, of how her silly romantic imagination had made up the beginning of a beautiful love story. Love—romance—— Tears welled up and rolled down her cheeks.

'Well,' he said contemptuously, '*what* did you think? And for God's sake turn off the tears, they don't impress me. You've made a fool of me—doesn't that satisfy you, without any further tricks?'

Amanda sniffed and swallowed. 'H-have you got a hand-kerchief, please?'

He looked hard at her, then went across the room, opened a drawer, and threw a folded white handkerchief in her direction. She grabbed it, blew her nose, wiped her eyes, and said tremulously, 'I just wanted you to kiss me again, that's all. And now, will you please go away while I put my dress on.'

For a moment he stood silent, frowning down at her. He was still naked to the waist, but now the strength of his body with the line of dark hair down his chest and the wide muscular shoulders did nothing but alarm her and she looked away quickly. 'Please go,' she said again.

He picked up his shirt from the floor and with one last, frowning look at her he went out of the room and closed the door behind him.

CHAPTER THREE

IT took Amanda one minute to get back into the hated cerise dress and zip it up with shaking hands. It took her ten minutes before she felt equal to going into the next room and facing Blair Craddock again.

In a corner of the bedroom was a built-in washing fitment and she stared at herself in the mirror with the utmost disgust. Tears had ploughed thin furrows in the heavy make-up on her cheeks and the black mascara that Elaine had plastered on her lashes had run into the furrows. She turned the taps on full, grabbed the soap, and worked up a fine lather, as if she could wash off all evidence of this lamentable evening. Even so, the traces of the mascara left black streaks on Blair's white towel. She glared at it, telling herself that it was his own fault, trying to hate him. But she couldn't keep it up. It hadn't really been his fault at all —it had been hers, her honesty admitted. She had submitted to being dressed up like a tart, and it was her own doing if she had been mistaken for one. Blair had said she had made a fool of him, but all she had done was to make a fool of herself.

But lengthy explanations weren't in order—he was too angry to bother with them and she was in no state to try to excuse herself. She would hold up her head and try to walk with dignity out of his apartment. And that, she thought dismally, would be the end of anything there might ever have been between them.

It was then that it came to her that the silver shoes were still in the next room where she had kicked them off, and you couldn't walk with dignity without shoes—not in this dress, anyway. She went to the door and opened it a little way. She could see the top of Blair's dark head resting against one of the linen-covered chairs. She said, 'May I have my shoes, please?'

He didn't move. He said quite calmly—all anger gone now—'Come and get them.'

They were lying close to his stretched-out legs. Hurriedly, not looking at him, she grabbed them and retired to the other side of the room to put them on.

Putting on shoes is not an easy thing to accomplish with dignity at the best of times, and Elaine's shoes were at least half a size too small for Amanda. Holding on to a chairback with one hand, she struggled ungracefully, nervously aware that Blair had turned his head and was watching her.

'Hadn't you better sit down?' he suggested when she had dropped the left shoe for the third time.

There was nothing else for it. She sat briefly and fixed both shoes. Then she got up and made for the door. She actually had hold of the handle when he said quietly, 'Amanda.'

There was a quality in the deep voice that riveted her. She stopped, motionless, not even looking round at him.

'Come back,' he said, and she did turn her head then. There was that expression on his face again—not quite a smile—that she had first seen in the party room before he walked across to her and Laurie. A gleam in the eye, a twitch of the muscles round his mouth. Hope rose as she thought—perhaps if I told him he would understand—we could start all over again——

She walked back and sat down stiffly on the chair opposite him, as he motioned her to it.

'Now then,' he said, 'I think you've got some explaining to do.'

She lifted her eyes briefly to his and dropped them again. 'Then you don't still think I'm a—a——' She found that she didn't even know the word for what he had thought of her.

'No,' he said. He regarded her scrubbed face and newly-combed hair thoughtfully. (It had been an effort to make herself use his comb, but now her silky hair fell as it had always done, youthfully, in a curving mink-fair drift on to her shoulders.) 'No,' he repeated, 'I've changed my mind. But I think you'd better cover that awful dress up. It bothers me. No, not that,' he added sharply as she stretched out for the blue silk wrapper she had worn before and had laid over the back of the chair she was sitting on. 'I'll find you something else.'

He whipped away the silk wrapper and went into the bedroom, emerging with an olive-green towelling robe which he draped round her shoulders as she sat there. Timidly she thrust her arms into the sleeves, which were inches too long, and covered her legs with the softly-looped fabric.

'That's better,' he said. 'Now, relax and tell me what you were playing at just now, when I rescued you from Laurie Fellowes's clutches. That smile was intended for me, surely?'

She looked down at her hands, twisting her fingers together. 'In a way.'

'And what might "in a way" mean?'

'Well——' She bit her lip. Hopeless to try to explain about the *Vogue* photograph, about her adolescent fantasies of the afternoon. 'Well—I just smiled. I—I thought I might have seen you before.'

'Oh yes?' The tone was heavily sarcastic.

'Yes, I did,' she said, on the defensive now. 'What's so wrong about smiling at someone?'

The dark brows rose cynically. 'Nothing—nothing at all. Except that naturally I took that smile as an invitation. You were one of Elaine's set—your dress, your hair, your general get-up——' he waved a hand '—it was obvious that you were available.'

She sat up straight. 'Well, I'm not!' she snapped, anger taking the place of her former mortification.

His lip twisted. 'You've made that abundantly clear.'

'And I'm not one of Elaine's set either,' she added.

He lay back in his chair. 'Then perhaps you'll tell me what the hell you're doing here. I think I deserve that much consideration.'

'I'm here to meet my father,' she said. 'He hasn't come back from Paris yet.'

She watched his face while that sank in. His expression didn't give much away, but she thought she had scored a point. At last he said, 'You're James's daughter? I knew he had a daughter, he was talking about it not long ago. But I thought he said she was a schoolgirl.'

'I *was* a schoolgirl until last Christmas.'

He stared at her. 'My God!' he said. He got up and went over to the cupboard to pour himself a drink. Then he came back and sat down again. He passed a hand across his wide brow. 'This is a facer,' he said. 'I suppose I should say I'm sorry, but I don't think there was any way I could have guessed that you weren't—what I took you for. And I usually accept what I'm offered'—the dark eyes twinkled wickedly—'if I'm in the mood and if the offer is tempting enough.'

Amanda looked at him coldly, although she was feeling anything but cold inside as she met that glitter in his eyes. 'How arrogant can you get? I didn't offer you anything.'

'My dear girl!' he expostulated. 'That smile of yours— you aren't going to sit there and tell me you don't know what effect it has on a man?'

'Smile?' She frowned, genuinely puzzled. 'I don't know what you're talking about.'

'Don't you?' he said sceptically. 'How old are you, Amanda?'

'Eighteen,' she said.

He ran a hand distractedly through his thick hair. 'Eighteen! And she goes about flashing smiles like that at men! James is going to have his work cut out with a daughter like you around the place.'

'I'm not going to be around the place. You don't think I intend to stay here, do you?'

'Don't you?'

'No, I don't. I don't like it. I don't like the house, I don't like the people here. I don't like anything about it.' Her voice rose rather wildly. 'I promised to come here to meet my father and as soon as I've met him I'm going home as quickly as I can.'

'And where's home?'

'A little village in South Devon. You wouldn't know it—it's not your sort of place.'

'And how do you know what my sort of place is?' he enquired.

She glanced at him uncertainly. 'Well, all this——' She gestured round the expensively-fitted apartment. 'And—and——'

'—and my shameful behaviour just now?' He grinned. He didn't look in the least ashamed. 'Even at eighteen I'd have thought you would have discovered that men are much the same wherever they happen to live, when there's a pretty girl around.'

'I think that's horrible,' she burst out hotly. 'There are other things besides——'

'Making love? Ah yes, many other things, but none of them quite so pleasant.' He was watching her closely. 'But I can see that you're bored with the whole subject. Suppose we talk about other things until your father turns up?'

'I don't want to talk about anything—with you,' she said, and knew even as she said it that it wasn't true. She wanted to talk to him about all sorts of things, to find out all about him—the things he liked, the books he read, and—most important of all—if he was married. As that revealing thought surfaced in her mind she said stiffly, 'I think I'd like to go back to my room.'

'Would you know how to get there?' he asked. 'This is a very confusing house to find your way around in. You wouldn't want to run into Laurie Fellowes again, would you?' he added wickedly.

She glared at him. 'I thought it was the least you could do to——'

'Oh no,' he interrupted. 'Don't count on me to solve your problems for you. Now, how about a friendly drink together?'

Her eyes widened and she started to get out of her chair. He sighed. 'Relax, Amanda, I was going to suggest a cup of tea. I make a very good cup of tea,' he added.

He stood up and put a finger under her chin, lifting her face to his, coaxing her to smile back at him, as if she were a sulky child. But she wasn't a child any longer. She had learned a lot in a very short time this evening—about the world, and people, and most of all about herself. The touch of his fingers on her skin was sending shivers flickering about inside her, but she wasn't going to let him know that. She removed his hand firmly, lifted her chin, and said with a certain dignity, 'Thank you, I should like a cup of tea very much.'

He stood watching her and his mouth was very gentle. 'I *do* mean tea, you know, not anything else.'

She said, surprised, 'Yes, of course you do—what else could you mean?'

He smiled. 'You really are an innocent, aren't you, Amanda? I fear for you in this great big wicked world.'

She tossed her hair back from her face. 'I'm learning fast,' she said. She stood up and followed him to the door of the small kitchen, but remained outside. The room was tiny, hardly larger than a cupboard, although it was—to a quick glance—equipped with all the most expensive modern gadgets. She would rather have liked to inspect them, but if she offered to help she would be much too close to him for her own peace of mind.

He reached up and took a rack of canisters from a cupboard. 'Darjeeling? Earl Grey? Lapsang Souchong? Something in a Chinese script that I can't read? What's your fancy?'

Amanda was busy adjusting the sleeves of the towelling gown and fixing the girdle so that she didn't trip over the hem. 'Where I come from,' she said, 'it's just called tea.'

The kettle boiled and he switched it off. 'Devon cream teas—home-made scones and strawberry jam? You must introduce me to that pleasure one of these days.'

She glanced at the tall figure inside the kitchen, elegant in well-cut dark trousers and silk shirt. It was difficult to imagine him tucking into a cream tea in a Devon farmhouse. Exotic foreign dishes and vintage wines seemed to fit better with his image.

He carried the tray through to the living room and put it down with a flourish on the low table beside the sofa. 'There! You see I *do* know how to entertain a lady with decorum if I put my mind to it.' He sat down and patted the sofa by his side. 'Sit down by me, Amanda, and be friendly. Just to show you forgive me. Otherwise I'll never be able to look James in the face when he gets here.'

He was keeping it light—doing his best to put her at ease. She drew the towelling robe round her legs and sat down beside him.

'What is your connection with my father?' she enquired, carefully avoiding touching his fingers as he handed her tea in a cup of eggshell blue. 'It seems silly, but I don't know what his business is. I don't really know anything at all about him. I'd almost forgotten he existed until last week, when the solicitor told me he wanted to see me.'

'Your parents were divorced?' It was a question. Obviously this man knew nothing of the circumstances.

She nodded. 'When I was a baby. My mother died soon afterwards and my grandmother brought me up. She died herself a few months ago; I suppose my father was told and that's when he suddenly had the idea that he wanted to see me after all these years.' She tried to keep the coldness out of her voice. She was doing her best not to nourish resentment, or to make any judgment of her father until she had met him, although the events of the day hadn't helped. 'What *is* his business?' she asked again.

Blair leaned back, cradling his cup in long, slender fingers. 'Well, he's the senior partner in our firm. Senior in age, I mean. He and my father ran the business together and when my father died some years ago I took over his share. We make textiles—Caradawc is the name. You may have heard of us.'

'Caradawc—yes, I have. I've seen advertisements, I remember the name because it's so unusual.'

'It's the Welsh form of Craddock. The family came from Wales originally and my grandfather, who started the business, thought we should hang on to the Welsh connection.' He grinned and added, 'Who'd remember Craddock Curtains—but Caradawc's a different matter. We were one of these highly-respected old manufacturing firms, trading on our good name, not making any spectacular profits—until your father came along. He teamed up with my dad, and after that everything took off. In a few years—with your father's know-how—the company was transformed, expanded, modernised, taken into world markets—the lot.'

Amanda stared thoughtfully into her cup. 'He sounds like a—a tycoon.'

Blair grinned. 'I suppose you could say that.'

'And you? Are you a tycoon too?'

His eyes narrowed. She had thought that they were almost black, but now she saw that they were blue, the darkest blue imaginable, and just now they had a steely glint. 'Do you always like to label people?' he said.

He was evidently still feeling sore about what had happened in the bedroom, but she wasn't going to let him shake her confidence by any small show of aggression. She said lightly, 'I didn't intend to label you, Mr Craddock, I'm merely trying to get the picture.'

'I see. And the name is Blair, by the way.'

She smiled. 'Don't you like people to be interested in you—Blair?'

The steely glint remained. 'You're right, Amanda, you are indeed learning fast,' he said grimly. 'And don't smile at me like that, there's a good girl. It has a very curious effect on me.'

She met his eyes and her heart lurched. Then her gaze dropped to his mouth and stayed there and, only half aware of what she was doing, she moved towards him on the sofa. She heard his quick catch of breath and his arm went round her, pressing her hard against him, pushing the dressing gown apart. His mouth hovered above hers. 'You *are* a little devil, you know, in spite of——'

There was a noise in the entrance lobby and a man's voice, tired and exasperated, called, 'Blair, are you there? I've just got back and there's this bloody party going on. I'm trying to find my daughter. Have you seen——'

A man's figure appeared in the doorway and he stood staring blankly at the couple on the sofa, while Blair removed his arm from around Amanda without haste and got to his feet. 'Hullo, James,' he said. 'Your daughter's here, safe and sound. We were just having some tea— come and join us.'

Amanda had purposely not tried to imagine what her father would look like because people never seemed to turn out like the picture you had made of them. But now she knew that she had had a vague image at the back of her mind of the tycoon who was the owner of this great, brash house: an image from a film, perhaps, of a large, square, grizzled man with red puffy cheeks, smoking a fat cigar. She almost laughed aloud now, because the reality was so very different. She could never have dreamed up this man who stood in front of her, this man with the thin, lined, clever face and sad brown eyes like monkey's eyes.

He didn't move or make any attempt to greet her. He just stood staring at her as she sat on the sofa, totally unable to move. Then he looked back at Blair, passing a hand across his brow where wiry brown hair was receding slightly. 'What the hell's going on here? What are you up to, Blair? My God, if you——' He took a step forward.

Blair put out a hand and gripped the other man's arm. 'Take a hold on yourself, man, nothing's going on. Amanda and I are sitting here getting to know each other. She got somewhat—disenchanted—with Elaine's party, so we decided to have one of our own while she waited for you to arrive.'

James Dawson shook his head quickly from side to side, as if he were trying to pull himself together, trying to clear everything out of his mind in order to make room for something new and important. 'You're Amanda,' he said questioningly, like a man not sure of his welcome, and she saw a kind of humility in the sad monkey eyes. He was waiting for her verdict.

She didn't know if she liked him or if she forgave him for the past, but in a sudden warm surge of compassion she saw that as well as apprehension there was a deadly tiredness in his face. She stood up and went across the room to him. 'Yes, I'm Amanda,' she said. And she reached up and kissed his cheek.

For a second he looked almost dazed, then he took both her hands and held them tightly, saying nothing, just looking at her as if he could never take his eyes off her. Shakily he passed a hand over his brow again. 'You'll have to forgive me, Amanda, you're rather a surprise. I think I was expecting a girl in a gym-slip with a hockey stick.'

The tension snapped and she grinned. 'I have both, back at home,' she said. 'Maybe I should have brought them.'

For the first time a smile flickered in the brown eyes. 'Not appropriate, I think. But I'd like to know why you're wearing Blair's dressing gown.'

She looked down at the towelling robe that enfolded her. 'I—I was——' She glanced helplessly at Blair, who had tactfully settled himself in a corner of the settee, removed from this family reunion, and had picked up a book.

He looked up. 'Your daughter was feeling the draught, James—in every sense of the term. She hadn't come equipped for an evening party and the elegant Mrs French fitted her up with a not-very-suitable dress. That's how it was, wasn't it, Amanda?'

She nodded. He had it all worked out, hadn't he? He knew half the story and he had accurately guessed the rest. There wasn't much that this man would miss, she thought with a qualm of dismay. It would be impossible to hold out against him—mentally, verbally, or—or physically, she added to herself, thinking with an inward shiver how easy it would have been for him to have taken what he wanted from her just now in the bedroom, however hard she had struggled.

'H'm,' said James, untying the girdle of the robe. 'Show me the dress.'

She slipped out of the gown and let it fall to the floor. The cerise dress clung—rather limply now—to her pretty figure, side slits gaping apart to disclose long, shapely legs in their sheer tights, the tassel hanging from the triangular hip-yoke with an unmistakable message.

James stared, transfixed. 'My God,' he breathed at last. 'I'll slay Elaine for this!'

Amanda got hastily back into the robe. 'Oh, it wasn't altogether her fault.' She didn't know quite why she had to rush to Elaine's defence; it was really to prevent her father losing his temper—he looked so dreadfully tired. 'You see, she hadn't——'

James shook his head. 'It's no use, Amanda, she should have known better. I spoke to her on the phone, I asked her to look after you until I could get here. It was quite unforgivable, dressing you up like that—pushing you into the middle of one of her God-awful parties.' Angry colour was dyeing the putty-pale cheeks and thick vertical grooves were settling between the brown eyes.

Amanda put a hand on his arm. 'Please!' she pleaded. 'Please don't be angry.' She didn't think she could take much more tonight; she turned away quickly as slow tears forced themselves under her lids.

'Oh, I'm sorry,' said James immediately. 'I'm sorry, Amanda. Forgive me, it's been a long day.' He slumped into a chair and closed his eyes.

Blair got up and stood looking down at him. 'I don't think tea's what you need, James. I've got some rather nice Cognac.'

There was silence in the room while Blair filled a glass and brought it back. James took a couple of gulps at the brandy and smiled faintly. 'That's better. Things get out of proportion sometimes.' He laid his head back and regarded the other two, standing above him. 'This is a pretty poor way of meeting, Amanda, so sorry. You're a lovely girl. She's a lovely girl, isn't she, Blair, my daughter?'

'I think so too,' said Blair gravely, his eyes on the girl beside him.

'And I've been all sorts of a fool, all these years, not knowing what she was like. Go on, tell me what a prize idiot I've been.'

Blair regarded Amanda with frank appreciation. 'You've certainly missed a trick or two, James, which isn't like you. Never mind, you can make up for it now she's here.'

She looked up and caught the mischievous glitter in the very dark blue eyes. How about all that I'm-going-home-as-soon-as-I-can stuff? he was asking. 'I don't think I like being discussed like a parcel in the lost property office,' she said lightly.

James pulled himself to his feet. 'She has spirit too,' he commented delightedly. 'We'll talk tomorrow, Amanda. Won't be human until I've had some sleep.' He put a hand on her shoulder and kissed her forehead. 'Goodnight, my dear. Go on looking after her, Blair, there's a good chap. You're doing a fine job,' he added with a faint grin. 'I'll be off—to bed.' He staggered slightly.

Blair took a step forward. 'You're O.K.? Shall I——?'

The older man waved him away. 'No, no, I'm all right. Fine in the morning.' He stopped for a moment, looking at Amanda with a kind of difficult intensity, as if he were willing his eyes to focus. 'Lovely,' he murmured. 'Lovely.' And he walked not very steadily out of the room and closed the door.

Amanda looked up at Blair with a little frown. 'Is he ill? Or——'

'He's not drunk, if that's what you're thinking,' he said crisply. 'He's been overdoing it recently, that's all. He'll have to rest again.'

'Again?'

He looked down at the table. 'The tea's probably gone cold by now,' he said. 'Shall we make some more?'

'What did you mean—*again*?' she insisted.

'Well, that's another thing he'd probably rather tell you himself. He was warned recently by his doctors that he had to slow down. It's quite impossible for James to slow down unless he's actually tethered to a post, so we persuaded him to have a fortnight in a convalescent home. He moaned about it, of course, but it did him a lot of good.' He picked up the tray. 'No more tea?'

She shook her head absently. 'No. No, thanks.'

Blair was regarding her quizzically. 'I can see that the tea party's over. Shall I escort madam to her room? I've no doubt we can track it down if we do it together, and if we encounter Laurie Fellowes or any of his kind on the way I can deal with them on your behalf.'

The dark blue eyes were dancing, and in spite of herself she began to smile. He took a step forward and put one strong finger across her lips. 'Careful!' he said. 'Careful, Amanda, remember what I told you.' He linked an arm loosely with hers, picked up the trailing hem of the robe as if it were a train, and led her out of the apartment.

The way to Amanda's room led along various passages and through a square lobby, from where could be heard laughter and talk from the party. 'They'll keep it up most of the night,' Blair said, 'and sleep most of tomorrow. What a life!'

'It wouldn't suit me,' said Amanda, pulling a face. 'But I'll be going home tomorrow.'

'Are you quite sure?' Blair said softly as they turned into another long corridor.

'Yes, quite sure,' she said firmly. 'This is my room, I think, this one at the end.' She opened the door a crack. 'Yes, this is right.' She went inside and switched on the light. Then she turned. 'Thank you, and——'

Blair had come in behind her and closed the door and now he stood with his back to it, hands nonchalantly in his pockets. The teasing look had gone from his eyes, leaving his face serious, oddly intense. A pang of something that felt like fear ran through Amanda's whole body and she took a step backwards.

'Don't worry,' he said grimly. 'Everything's under control. I just want to say that I regret some of the happenings of the evening. Not all, but some.' He was looking at her intently. 'Just forget about the whole thing, Amanda, it was all a mistake.' He smiled then. 'Goodnight, kitten. Sleep well.' The door opened behind him and swiftly he was gone.

'But—but your dressing gown—don't you want it——?' She opened the door, but he was nowhere in sight. He must have almost run away, she thought. He couldn't get away from me quickly enough. The thought made her feel vaguely depressed.

The room depressed her too. It was beautiful and luxurious, of course, like she imagined a room in a top hotel might be, but there was none of the cosiness that a bedroom should have. Dispiritedly, Amanda got undressed and into the chiffon nightdress that Elaine had left for her. Then, because it was somehow comforting and familiar, she wrapped herself in Blair's dressing gown again and got into bed. Her watch told her that it was past midnight, but she didn't feel sleepy. It had been such a strange day and so much had happened, and she felt stirred up inside.

From the distance came the faint sound of the party, still going on, and she had a picture of the big, smoke-hazy room and the avid faces round the gaming table. No, it wasn't her scene, she could never be happy here, and she would have to tell her father that, when they talked tomorrow. She wasn't sure whether he would want her to stay, but she had to be prepared.

Inevitably the thought of Blair Craddock came into her mind. If she left tomorrow she wouldn't see him again, and perhaps that was just as well. He was a sophisticated man of the world and she wasn't in his league. His lovemaking had shaken her to the depths, his kiss had awakened dizzy whirlpools of desire that she hadn't even suspected were there. But what to her had been a new, shattering experience had been to him nothing more than a pleasant interlude leading up to—as it had turned out—nothing at all! Of course he had been angry and disappointed. He was a virile man—there was a primitive, masculine ruthlessness under that suave, mocking manner of his. He would want a woman whose experience would match his own. A little kitten from a Devon village would just be a joke.

Yes, much better that she didn't see him again.

As she lay there in the soft bed, her hands behind her head, her eyes became very large and dreamy. But she *had* disturbed him a little. Even after he found out who she was he had said, 'Don't smile at me like that, it has a very curious effect on me.'

With a little sigh she drew Blair's dressing gown closer round her; the texture felt slightly rough against the smoothness of her skin. 'Forget about the whole thing, Amanda,' he had said.

Amanda stretched out and switched off the light.

And remembered.

When she finally slept she slept soundly and wakened to find Mrs Fogg standing beside the bed with a tray in her hands, and the morning sun slanting through the venetian blind on to her small neat figure in its bottle-green overall.

Amanda blinked and pushed the hair out of her eyes and was suddenly aware that she was still wearing Blair's dressing gown. 'Goodness, I've overslept,' she said confusedly, wondering what Mrs Fogg would think of a girl who goes to bed in a man's dressing gown.

But if Mrs Fogg noticed anything unusual she ignored it. 'Not really, miss, it's only half past ten. Not late for *this* house!' She sniffed. 'Most of 'em won't be stirring for hours yet.' She put the tray down on the bedside table. 'Your father sent a message, will you meet him in the drawing room in an hour, Miss Dawson. He wants to take you out to lunch, which I must say is very thoughtful of him, there being a fair lot to do in the way of clearing up, and Iris from the village not arriving yet.'

Amanda sat up. 'Yes. Yes, of course. And thank you for bringing my breakfast. I could have got up, though. I don't want to give you extra work.'

The woman regarded her with bright, knowing eyes. 'It's all right so long as it's for *you*, miss. There's some as I wouldn't do it for, not if they paid me double,' she added darkly.

Amanda lifted her eyebrows as the door closed behind Mrs Fogg. No need to wonder who that broadside was directed at. Elaine French was certainly not popular with that lady.

Nor with me, she thought, attacking scrambled egg on toast with appetite. Which is just one of the reasons why

I'm going back to Devon today. That thought brought Blair Craddock into her mind—not that he had been very far away from it since the first moment she saw him—and she continued to think about him as she finished the egg and went on to toast and honey and piping hot coffee. When she got out of bed, finally, and slipped off his dressing gown she felt somehow forsaken. She touched it with her fingers as it lay on the bed and she began to wonder how she was going to return it to him. She certainly didn't intend to go wandering about searching for Blair's private apartment. In fact, she didn't intend to see him again before she left, if she could help it. It was a little easier to be firm about that in the clear light of morning than it had been last night when she went to sleep. The man-in-the-background was going to be relegated to the shadows as fast as she could put him there, she assured herself, and went on repeating it while she bathed and dressed in the demure grey suit and white blouse she had arrived in yesterday. A light make-up, a touch of pink lipstick, her fair hair smooth and shining on her shoulders, and she was ready.

She regarded herself in the mirror with a faintly mocking smile. 'A little kitten from the country, that's what you are,' she told her reflection, and went to look for her father.

After taking a wrong turning and ending up in a garden room, she found him at last, standing by the window of the big drawing-room, surrounded by the debris of last night's party—the overflowing ashtrays, the glasses lying around on the floor as well as the tables, the baize-covered gaming table looking incredibly squalid, somehow, in the morning sunlight that poured in through the long windows. She stood in the doorway for a moment, watching him, noticing the droop of the shoulders under his brown tailored jacket, the way his hands hung limply at his side, the deeply-etched lines on his face. He couldn't yet be fifty, but he looked an old man, and suddenly Amanda felt a pull at her heart.

She went forward quickly. 'Hullo—good morning,' she said, and smiled at him.

He turned and it was as if all the cares of the world had fallen away. He took both her hands in his and smiled back at her. 'Now I can really look at you,' he said, his eyes going delightedly over her clear cheeks touched with pink, her shining hair, and the grey suit with the white bow of the blouse collar hugging her neck.

'Yes,' he said, mock-solemn, 'I was right; you are quite the most delightful and wholesome thing I've seen around this house for a long, long time.'

'Thank you.' A dimple appeared in Amanda's left cheek. 'Although I'm not too sure that wholesome is a word that most girls would appreciate these days. It suggests sewing samplers and governesses and being-seen-and-not-heard, wouldn't you say?'

'I was thinking more of tea on the lawn, and tennis parties, and strawberries and cream.'

She gave him an old-fashioned look. 'Ah, but you didn't hear what the nice young ladies got up to in the shrubbery, did you?'

He chuckled. 'You do me good, Amanda. I feel better already. We'll go out to lunch and you can tell me all about yourself.'

At that moment a woman drifted into the room and made her way towards them. Amanda vaguely remembered her from last night as a large, quite handsome woman with bright yellow hair, but this morning she looked a wreck. She wore a faded wrapper, her hair straggled down across puffy cheeks, and without its foundation garment her body was a sagging mountain of flesh.

She stared blearily at them. 'James! Bright and early, aren't we?' The effort to be gaily facetious was repellent. 'Too bad you weren't here last night, you missed a real sw-swinging party.'

'Fortunately,' rejoined James coldly.

The woman gave a high titter. 'You like your little joke, don't you, James? I was jus' going to have a quick one—that all right by you?' She gazed longingly towards the littered bar.

'Help yourself,' said James without cordiality. He turned to Amanda and took her by the arm. 'Come on, let's get out of here before any more of them come crawling out from under their stones.' They went together through the open patio windows and along the front of the house. James's mouth was set in disgust. 'I should have put a stop to these parties of Elaine's ages ago, I suppose. I dunno'—he hunched his shoulders wearily—'it just didn't seem worth the trouble.' His voice changed, became positive. 'But now that you're here things are going to be quite different. I won't have you exposed to that sort of party. I shudder to think what might have happened last night if Blair hadn't found you and taken you under his wing.'

Amanda thought with a glimmer of humour: You'd shudder even more if you knew what actually did happen! No, that wasn't fair. If Blair had known who she was from the beginning none of it would have happened. With a sudden flash like the bursting of hundreds of sky-rockets the thought came: But oh, I'm glad it did.

Her father was talking again, looking wry. 'I admit I did have a qualm or two when I first saw you and Blair on the settee with you in his dressing gown. It looked like what used to be called a compromising situation. But of course I should have known that Blair wouldn't be likely to let me down.'

She glanced up at him as they walked over the grass together. 'Let *you* down?' Her mouth twitched and the dimple showed. 'Wouldn't I have been in the act too?'

He studied her face, not smiling now. 'You're a lovely girl, Amanda, lovely enough to tempt any man to the limit, as I expect you've already found out.' She heard the question in his voice although he didn't say the words. She didn't have to account for her actions, she thought; he had relinquished any possible claim on her confidence. Still, he *was* her father.

'If you're asking me whether I've—I've been made love to, then I haven't,' she said. 'And I certainly didn't tempt Mr Craddock to the limit, if that's what you're thinking.'

'No, no,' he said hastily, but she thought he sounded pleased. 'It was only a mistaken impression. Blair's no plaster saint—to use an out-of-date expression—but you're very young, and you're my daughter, and Blair and I are friends as well as partners. And then, of course, there's Juliet.'

'His wife?' she asked quickly. She had to say it quickly or she couldn't have said it at all. A huge heavy lump seemed to have settled in the region of her throat.

James shook his head. 'Not yet,' was all he said, but it was enough.

They had reached the garages now and Fogg was there with his head under the bonnet of the limousine. He lifted it out and said, 'Good morning, sir, good morning, miss.'

' 'morning, Fogg. Feel like taking us out to Shevely for lunch?' asked James cheerfully. And to Amanda, 'It's a favourite pub of mine in the next village. They do quite a good steak.'

Fogg ushered them into the softly-cushioned back seat as if they were royalty. As they drove down the winding drive and out into the country lanes Amanda looked out of the car window, seeing nothing. So—Blair was engaged, or as good as engaged, which was only to be expected, she assured herself. It was quite ridiculous to have this numb, desolate feeling. She had been into all that this morning and decided quite reasonably that the best thing to do was to remove herself from his sphere as quickly as possible before she found herself with a problem she couldn't cope with.

'How do you like our Cotswold country, Amanda?' her father was saying.

She blinked and focussed on the scenery, green and lush and somehow reassuring because it still was a little like Devon—her part of Devon, anyway.

'Lovely,' she said. If the circumstances had been different she wouldn't have minded contemplating the exchange. To live in one of the rather beautiful cottages of honey-grey stone which looked as if they had grown into the landscape, but not at Radneys. A house like Radneys should never have been put here, like a stiff, exotic orchid in the middle of a country garden of delphiniums and roses and marigolds.

Shevely, when they got there a few minutes later, turned out to be quite a large village with a long main street. Cottages and shops and mellowed old houses jostled each other along the length of the street, which divided half way to accommodate a stone building with arcades. 'The old market hall,' James explained. 'The locals are very proud of their history. Also, on the hard-headed side, it brings in the tourists.' He nodded towards the rows of parked cars along one side of the street and the small groups of sightseers with cameras and guide-books. 'There's an interesting ancient church, I believe—I haven't seen it myself—and a museum full of butter-churns and Toby jugs. The Cotswolds are very much geared to the tourist trade—all good for business,' he added with a grin.

The car pulled up before a weathered stone building which looked as if some squire had once lived there, but which now sported a discreet board saying 'Shevely Arms Hotel, A.A., R.A.C.' in gold letters on a blue background.

'Give us a couple of hours, Fogg,' instructed James, helping Amanda out of the car, and the chauffeur touched his cap and drove off.

Inside, the hotel was half period piece, half sheer luxury. Massive ceiling beams, tiny windows set into incredibly thick walls, dark wood from forests long since dead; all this set off by ankle-thick carpets, glittering glass chandeliers lighting an interior that must always resist the daylight, deep lounges, a horseshoe bar with a mirror-backing which effectively doubled the number of bottles on the polished glass shelves.

James glanced at his watch. 'I ordered lunch when I phoned; it should be coming up any moment.'

The lounge-bar was about half full of prosperous-looking customers—some women, but mostly men; dressed in expensive 'country' clothes and all talking very loudly. 'Let's go in here,' said James, leading the way to a table in a sort of cubbyhole enclosed on three sides by high wooden screens. 'I don't take to the set who patronise this place— too much money and not enough to do, and all fancying themselves as landed gentry. Although I suppose,' he added, pulling a wry face, 'that the same might be said of me, except that I'm not the idle type.'

Amanda studied his face as they sat down. No, she thought, you're certainly not the idle type. There was an urgency, a drive about him that was in no way belied by the sad monkey-eyes; he was a high-tension person, she had seen that last night, even when he had been so tired.

White-coated waiters were moving around, but the man who approached wore a well-cut lounge suit in pin-stripe. Probably the manager, Amanda thought. Her father would no doubt be an important and valued customer.

He greeted James with friendly deference and said that lunch would be ready shortly. 'Can I get you a drink, Mr Dawson?' He looked appreciatively at Amanda.

James ordered a whisky. 'And for my daughter——?' He consulted Amanda and seemed quite pleased when she said she would like a tomato juice. When the drinks had been brought he leaned back and beamed at her.

'Well, this *is* nice.' He shook his head wonderingly. 'How I could have been such a fool! What I've missed all these years, dashing about making money, when all the time I had a daughter like you!'

She smiled at him, a little embarrassed, sipping her tomato juice. He was going to ask her to stay, she was almost sure of that now, and she didn't know what she was going to say, how she was going to get out of it without being rude and hurtfully blunt. She couldn't say, as she had said to Blair Craddock last night, that she hated the house Radneys, and the whole style of life it stood for; even less could she admit that she needed to get as far away from Blair himself as possible, before she fell hopelessly (and hopelessly was the operative word!) in love with the man.

She looked up and round her at the wooden screens enclosing them. 'This is like our little church at home,' she said, playing for time. 'It's very old and some of the pews still have high wooden partitions all round, and a door. There's a story that in the old days the squire used to bring his friends and shut the door and they would play cards while the sermon was going on.'

James was watching her face. 'You're attached to your village and the home you've had with your grandmother, Amanda?'

She wondered if that were a loaded question. 'Oh yes, I love it,' she said quickly. 'I've been very happy there.'

'But you wouldn't want to rush back there straight away, would you?' Yes, it *had* been a loaded question. She hesitated and he went on eagerly, leaning forward in his chair, 'There's no point in trying to lead up to this cleverly, Amanda. The truth is, I want you to stay with me now I've found you. Just for a little while, until you marry and make a home of your own—which I've no doubt you will do before long. You're not'—he grimaced—'tied up to any country lad, are you?'

She shook her head slowly. 'No, but——' She met his eyes, the sad monkey-eyes, and thought, I could like him. There's something about him—and he *is* my father after all. To gain time she said, 'I don't really understand why you should suddenly want to see me, after all these years.'

'That's easy to explain, if not to justify. Recently my doctors sent me off to a nursing home to rest.' He pulled a face. 'It's wonderful how enforced idleness gives one a new perspective on things. In the mad rush of life you just go on and on and never have time to stop and think. Well, I had time then. And what I thought about was the daughter I didn't know, and I felt I must see her—while there was still time.'

'Still time?' Her eyes opened very wide. 'You're not really ill—you're not——?'

'Going to die just yet? I sincerely hope not, especially as I've just found you, Amanda, which has given me something to live for. You know, you're the only good thing that's happened to me for a long, long time.'

It wasn't fair, she thought, he was deliberately beginning to shackle her. What did they call it—the web of pity? She took refuge in lightness. 'Oh, surely not? James Dawson, the rich man! With a house like Radneys and an apartment in town, with a limousine and a chauffeur and an office with dozens of minions hurtling round doing your bidding, I bet!'

He smiled crookedly. 'Yes, I know, it sounds wonderful. The crock of gold at the end of the rainbow. What I've driven towards all my life. And it turned out pretty base metal—I guess it always does if you've let more worthwhile things go hang while you're clawing your way up. I'm not very good at grovelling, Amanda, and you're no doubt thinking that I don't deserve much consideration, after the way things have been, but—well, I'm asking. Pleading, if you like. Stay around for the rest of the summer, just so that we can get to know each other. Then, come the autumn, go back to your village if you must.'

She tried to think. Most girls would give a good deal for what she was being offered—luxury, the good life, to be spoiled and petted and indulged. She could imagine very well how it would be. Why didn't it appeal to her? She shook her head helplessly. 'I—I don't know——'

The manager came up to their table. 'There's a call for you from your home, Mr Dawson. Will you take it?'

A look of extreme irritation crossed his face; then he stood up. 'Will you excuse me, Amanda? I'd better go and see what it is, I won't be long.'

She watched him cross the lounge. Near the bar he stopped to speak to a man who was standing with his back to her. She watched them idly, then her heart gave a leap and started to thump wildly as she saw who it was. She could recognise Blair Craddock even without seeing his face: the width of his shoulders, the way his near-black hair grew into his neck. Under the glitter of the chandelier there was a reddish sheen on his hair that she hadn't noticed last night in the dim lights of his apartment. He wore a formal, dark grey suit that fitted impeccably across the back and down the elegant long length of him.

James said something and they both turned and looked over towards her. Instinctively she shrank back into her chair as if she was being threatened. Then her father walked on and Blair was coming towards her.

He dropped into the chair that James had vacated. 'Good morning, Amanda. You had a good night, I hope, after all your adventures.'

'Good morning, Mr Craddock. Yes, thank you, I slept very well.' She managed to keep her voice steady and very cool.

His brows rose a fraction and she saw that he had duly noted her chilly formality. He said, 'Your father invited me to join you both for lunch; I only wish I could, but I'm on my way to London to keep an appointment. James says he's been trying to persuade you to stay with him. Are you going to?'

She made herself meet his eyes and saw with a small

shock that instead of the indifferent politeness she expected to see there he looked serious, almost anxious.

She hedged. 'I—I don't know, I haven't made up my mind.'

He leaned forward and deliberately covered her hands with his. 'Please decide to stay, Amanda,' he said. 'You told me last night that nothing would induce you to stay, but please change your mind.'

She stammered, 'I—I don't really see what it can possibly mean to you, Mr Craddock.'

'Blair,' he said.

There was a very long pause. His eyes held hers and she began to feel that she was slowly becoming unable to breathe. At last he said, 'It *does* mean something to me, Amanda. I think you'd be surprised if you knew how much.'

She stared at him blankly, startled into silence. For a moment longer he sat quite still, his hand warm and hard on hers. Then he stood up abruptly. 'I must go,' he said. 'Au revoir, Amanda. And please make it "au revoir".'

She sat looking down dumbly at her hands, where his own had held them, and when she lifted her eyes again he had gone.

CHAPTER FOUR

'But Amanda must have a better room than this. Why, for goodness' sake, did you put my daughter in here, Elaine?'

James stood in the doorway of the room where Amanda had passed last night and fired the question at Mrs French. A very different Mrs French today; Amanda, standing on the other side of her father, noticed that Elaine had managed to erase, or at any rate cover up, what ravages last night's party must surely have left on her face. Only the whites of her eyes, dull and yellowish, showed that she had spent an unhealthy evening and a very short night. But she was carefully dressed now, in a stylish smoke-grey dress with thin silver chains at her neck and wrist, and her orange-coloured hair was brushed into a becomingly soft style. She was also making a determined show of being a good hostess, which effort, Amanda decided, must be for James's benefit and not for hers.

'Yes, I was *so* sorry——' she spread out her hands, dividing her apologies between James and Amanda. 'It really was too bad, but I explained to Amanda—didn't I, dear?—that if only I'd known before, I could have had one of the large rooms ready for her. But the dear child was expecting to meet you in London, James, and when you decided that Fogg should drive her here instead it took us *all* by surprise, and as we had already got the rooms fixed up for the party guests we just had to do the best we could. But the white room is vacant now, James, and of course Amanda can have that if she cares.'

'Ah, that's better.' He seemed satisfied with the explanation. 'You can move your things in then, Amanda.'

But he seemed reluctant to move from her side. He had

been like this ever since the moment over lunch in Shevely when she had told him that she would stay with him for the rest of the summer—like a man who has rubbed a magic lamp and had his dearest wish granted and who is now half afraid that it will disappear into thin air again.

Amanda looked into the small room and saw the toiletries arranged on the dressing table, the flimsy nightdress folded on the bed. And—Blair's olive-green dressing gown hanging over the back of a chair. 'No, really,' she said quickly, 'I'd rather not move. I like this room, it's just the right size for me.' And it was from the window here that she had first seen Blair. 'And anyway,' she went on before her father could persuade her, 'I haven't any things to move. I didn't expect to be staying and I didn't bring any clothes or anything with me.'

James nodded. 'No, of course, I forgot that. Oh well, if you're happy here, my dear, I suppose it's all right, is it?'

She smiled at him and his thin face with the sad brown eyes suddenly lit up. It was a terrible responsibility, she thought, being the object of another person's sole ambition in life. For that was how he had put it himself when they talked over lunch. 'I've just driven on regardless, Amanda,' he had confessed, 'because I suppose that's the way I'm made. I've got all the material things and the success, but I found out, when I was stuck away in that nursing home, that the material things aren't much good if you've nobody to care for, to give things to. I'm just ambitious for you now, my dear, to see you happy and fulfilled.' He had grinned at her almost sheepishly. 'And now, having wallowed sufficiently, I promise I won't bore you with any more of my soul-searchings. There's nothing so tedious as other people's guilty consciences.'

Standing beside him now in the wide corridor, with Elaine French watching her, Amanda said composedly, 'I'm quite all right, thank you, James.'

'Good. Splendid.' He gave her shoulder a little pat.

'When you've settled in we'll go round the place together. I'll wait for you in the drawing room.'

Elaine's sweet smile lasted until he had turned the corner, then the waspishness returned. 'So you're calling him James, are you? I'd have thought Daddy would have been more to the point. Sugar-Daddy!' Her face was a sneering mask. 'I suppose you think you're on to a good thing, Miss Amanda Dawson, but let me inform you——'

Amanda put her hands over her ears. 'Please stop!' The woman stared at her and unaccountably the flood of spiteful words dried up. The mouth closed peevishly, the bleary eyes narrowed, and altogether she looked so ugly and unattractive that Amanda felt something like pity for her.

She said impulsively, 'Look, Mrs French, I'm sorry you don't like me, but I'm afraid you'll have to put up with me for a month or two. I've promised my father to stay for the rest of the summer. I just want to say that I certainly won't interfere with you or the running of the house or anything at all. It would have been nice if we could have been friends, but——' she paused doubtfully.

Mrs French laughed. It wasn't a friendly sound and it seemed to say all there was to be said.

Amanda sighed and shrugged. She had done her best and there didn't seem to be anything more she could do at present. 'Oh well——'

Elaine French pushed the bedroom door open further and stood aside with an ironic gesture. 'Do make yourself at home—*dear*. I'm sure you will,' she added nastily, and walked away.

Amanda went into the bedroom. Her knees felt weak and her heart was beating quickly. She hated aggression, but she had learned already that it is fatal to give in tamely to it. She had no idea at all of the effect her clear, blue-grey gaze had on the aggressor; she had merely found that the only way to deal with unprovoked hostility was to meet it head-on.

Was her father really going to marry this woman, she wondered with a pang, and had he any idea what she was really like, or did she only show to him the sugar-sweet front she had put on just now? That was something she would have to find out for herself. She sighed. There were so many things to learn—a whole new way of life to discover. It was a daunting prospect.

She examined the bedroom with more interest now that it was going to be hers for the next few months. It *was* a nice room, she thought, admiring the burgundy-red bed-cover that made a dramatic touch with the white curly carpet and the wallpaper embossed with flower-clusters to match the bed-cover. The white curtains were superb—Caradawc, probably, as was the bed-cover. She crossed the room to examine them.

'Admiring our new line?' came James's laughing voice from the doorway. He had drifted back, unable, it seemed, to let her out of his sight for long.

'They're beautiful,' said Amanda, stroking the silky texture with gentle fingers. 'So clever to make a pattern with nothing but white. I suppose the pattern shows up because the weave goes in different directions, and some of it's glossy and some of it's matt. Fascinating!'

James came across the room to her, looking pleased. 'Somebody's been telling you all about our company's product? I wondered if you knew.'

'Well, just a bit about it. Blair told me last night.' She realised with horror that her cheeks were turning crimson. 'When—when we were waiting for you to arrive.' She rushed on, 'He told me it was a textile firm and that it was your doing that the name Caradawc is so well know today.'

James smiled. 'Nice of him, but let's say it's a corporate effort. Three of us involved at the top—Blair is in charge of the actual weaving and processing, Juliet is the wizard behind the designs. and I—more mundane but necessary— look after the sales side of the business.'

Amanda nodded, turning her head away. 'I see. I'd like to learn more about it all.' I'd like to see this Juliet, whom Blair is on the point of marrying. Perhaps if I saw them together, if I felt sure that they were in love, then it would be easier to get over this insane longing to see him again, to touch him, to hear his voice.

'That would be splendid,' James was saying enthusiastically. 'We'll show you over the mills one day soon. Our main place isn't far from here—a few miles from Stroud. Which is why I bought Radneys some years ago; it's handy for me, and Blair has his own part of the house, which seems to suit him very well. Of course, my wife was still alive when we came here. You knew I'd married again?'

How much was she supposed to know? It was awkward, being James's daughter and yet knowing almost nothing about him, whether he had loved his second wife, had been grief-stricken at her death—— 'I——' she began '—yes, Mrs French told me that she was your sister-in-law and that her sister had died in an accident last year. I'm—I'm so sorry.'

His face hardened. He said, 'It should never have happened.' He suddenly looked weary, hunching his shoulders and rubbing the back of his neck. 'So many things have happened in my life that shouldn't have happened,' he said. Then he brightened. 'But I feel somehow that I may have been let off the hook now. Reborn, I believe is the word.' He chuckled and his sad monkey-eyes were mischievous. 'Some baby!' he grinned.

He took hold of her arm. 'Come along, my dear, let me show you round my domain and then you can tell me what you think of it.'

Half an hour later the guided tour—as James called it— ended beside the swimming pool. 'Well,' he said, 'what do you think of Radneys?'

'It's—it's absolutely breathtaking,' Amanda replied carefully. She hadn't really changed her feeling about the enormous, cleverly-designed modern house, but her father must surely be proud of it and she wouldn't want to criticise.

He pulled out two loungers for them and they sat down. His eyes were quizzical. 'You don't think much of it, do you?'

'Oh!' she gasped. 'Is that how it seemed? I wouldn't for the world——'

'No, of course you wouldn't, you're a kind child, but we may as well get this clear from the start, my dear. I've asked you to leave your world and come into mine, which is different. Not better, but different. Please don't feel you have to be tactful about things in it that don't appeal to you; that would never do. Some of the joy of having you with me will be to find out about you—your likes and dislikes, your opinions and ideas about life and people. A fresh outlook on life is just what I need. Now come on, what's your true feeling about Radneys?'

She looked towards him doubtfully. They were sitting in the shade of a low, cedarwood shelter; at their feet the sunlight was dazzling as it reflected off the pale turquoise water in the pool and the surrounding white tiles; beyond, the gardens stretched away on all sides, perfectly designed, beautifully tended. From her chair she glimpsed the distant forms of two gardeners about their work. She said, 'I suppose I just feel—overwhelmed by a house like this. In our cottage in Kings Holton we could hardly swing a cat. Here there's room to swing a whole zoo if you wanted to.' She heard his chuckle and went on more confidently, 'Please don't think I don't like Radneys, but I think I was expecting something more—more in keeping with the countryside. Something older, perhaps, and more—more homely,' she finished rather lamely.

James was nodding thoughtfully. 'Fair comment,' he said. 'And I'm not sure I don't agree with you. Radneys was my wife's choice. We needed a house somewhere around here and I left it to her to find one. Radneys had just come on to the market—it had been built quite a short time before by some big American industrialist who'd decided to go back to the U.S.—and Deirdre fell in love with it. She was very social,' he added, and his expression was unreadable. 'Loved giving parties and having friends up here from London. The house was usually full. Her sister, Elaine, made her home here and I was glad for Deirdre to have her company when I was away from home—which was pretty often. Another point in Radneys' favour was that there was a separate wing for Blair. We work pretty closely together and that was a great convenience for us both. Of course it won't be big enough for him when he marries.'

Suddenly the sun went behind a cloud. 'Will that be soon?' Amanda made herself ask. Over the side of the low chair her hand touched the white tiles surrounding the swimming pool and they felt smooth and cold.

'No idea,' James smiled. 'Blair's a cagey type in his personal life, and I respect that. But he and Juliet seem to have something going for them and at a guess I'd say neither of them is the casual kind who would want an impermanent affair. Juliet's a lovely girl, I want you to meet her. She's in London just now. I thought you might like to come up with me tomorrow and then you could buy yourself the clothes and things you need.'

London—Juliet was there. And Blair was in London too. Amanda said hurriedly, 'Oh, but I must go back to the cottage first. All my clothes are there and—and there's the lease falling due soon and I suppose Gran's furniture will have to be sold, and——' All of a sudden the future presented mountains of complications. Only a few minutes ago she had thought she would like to meet this Juliet girl and now she was offered the opportunity she found herself making excuses, however valid, to go back to Devon.

James said, almost casually, 'Why not let me do something about the lease? It could probably be renewed and then you could keep on the cottage for the time being, and deal with things there later on.'

Amanda's eyes brightened. It would be wonderful to know that the cottage was still there for her to go back to (she wouldn't use the word 'escape' even in her thoughts) if everything here got too difficult. And James was showing her that he didn't want her to feel tied to him, that he wanted her to be free. That was generous of him.

'Oh, would you?' she said. 'That would be very kind.'

'Kind!' He waved the word away. 'I'll get in touch with my solicitors about it straight away, then you won't have to worry about the furniture and so on.' He felt in his pocket for a silver case and selected a cigar from it. 'You were very fond of your grandmother, weren't you?'

'Yes, I was. She was very good to me.' Gran had been strict—old-fashioned, really. She had never come through the barrier into the modern world, and never would have done although she had only been in her sixties when she died. 'Be in by ten o'clock, won't you, dear?' and 'Where are you going?' and 'Who have you been with?' Amanda had never really minded the loving concern, but now she saw that she might, eventually, have begun to feel stifled by it.

'Did she ever speak to you—about me?' asked James, examining the end of his cigar.

'No, not really. She used to talk a lot about my mother, but I didn't remember her either, of course. I was only about two when she died.'

He nodded slowly. 'All in the past. It seems such a long time ago. Some day we'll talk about it, but not now. Enough to say that I was at fault, I and my burning need to succeed, that was what caused the rift. But just let me say this for now, Amanda, and then we'll put it behind us for the time being. I *did* want very much to keep in contact with you, to see you from time to time as I could have done under the divorce settlement. I thought about it for a long time before I decided that it was fairer to you not to involve you in my rackety existence. And it *was* fairly rackety for years while I was working my way to where I am now, believe me.' His mouth pulled wryly. 'So all I could do was provide as best I could for your creature comforts, and leave you to grow up in your native climate. You never wanted for anything?'

She shook her head vehemently. 'No, never. The only thing was——'

'Yes?'

'I don't think Gran was really fair to you. I suppose you made some sort of settlement after the divorce, but you must have sent a good deal for extra money for me on top of that. She——she let me think that *she* was giving me all the little luxuries I had.'

James said rather bleakly, 'Your grandmother never liked or approved of me, and who could blame her? What she did was fairly natural, I think, and anyway we've got it straight now.' He grinned his lopsided grin. 'One small point in my favour, perhaps? I realise that I have to earn your——regard, right from square one.'

Amanda smiled shyly. 'I think you're up to square three already,' she said, and James gave a sudden shout of laughter.

'Great!' he cried. 'Great!'

Seeing his delighted smile, the way the lines smoothed themselves out on his tired face, she thought, 'Gosh, I've done it now——I've committed myself good and proper.' But in the rewarding glow of giving pleasure to another person, she couldn't manage to regret it. She was even able, for a short space of time, to push the thought of Blair Craddock back into the background where it ought to be. Blair, and the beautiful, clever, artistic, altogether wonderful menace that was called Juliet.

Amanda sat with her father at a corner table in a small, well-appointed restaurant near Piccadilly next day and tried to immerse herself in the unfamiliar surroundings and forget that they were expecting Blair to join them for lunch.

All the way up to London in the train this morning she had chatted to James, answering his questions about her school, the college, her friends, and at the back of her mind she had been rehearsing how she would behave when she met Blair again. She would be friendly, pleasant, but no more. At all costs she would avoid letting him see that what had happened between them at Radneys the night before last had meant anything more to her than a casual encounter—highlighted, perhaps, because of the misunderstanding and the rather unusual circumstances. She had remembered with shame how eagerly she had responded to his kisses—until she saw where they were leading—and wondered if he would remember, too, and be bored by the prospect of a naïve teenager with a crush on him. If, indeed, he had given the matter another thought—which he probably hadn't, she decided sadly.

As to the way he had spoken to her in the hotel at Shevely and his apparent eagerness for her to accept James's invitation to stay on at Radneys—well, that was probably just politeness. She couldn't let herself believe that he was really concerned one way or the other.

A waiter placed an enormous menu-card in front of her and she turned to James, after one baffled look at it. 'You choose, please,' she said, and while he conferred with the waiter her gaze moved round the dining room and she found herself appreciating the air of quiet luxury, the glitter of glass and cutlery, the tiny bouquets of pinks and miniature roses on the smooth, white-clothed tables, the mingled smells of cigars, elegantly turned-out women wearing subtle perfumes, and good food. It was quite a change from the Wimpy bar where she usually lunched with her friends from the college. But a nice change! With a rueful little sigh she reflected how easy it was to get used to being a rich man's daughter.

'There's Blair now!' said James, and Amanda's inside

lurched alarmingly. Watch it! she told herself, and fixed a friendly little smile on her mouth.

He was standing just inside the doorway, looking around the room. She saw him for a moment before he spotted their table and in that moment everything and everyone dissolved in a haze and there was only Blair, tall and lithe in his dark suit, with his black hair brushed to a sheen and the gleam in his eyes that seemed always to be savouring some private joke.

He had spotted them now and was making his way between the tables towards them. 'Hullo, Amanda—James. Well met, you two.'

It was quite an effort to look up and meet his eyes and smile in a friendly, pleasant way that put miles between them, when all the time she was gripping her table-napkin on her knee to stop her hands from shaking. It was terrifying, this purely physical response. Infatuation, she told herself, not love. Infatuation, they said, was like the measles—you got over it, sooner or later.

He sat down on Amanda's left and the waiter returned to the table. 'I've ordered Lobster Thermidor for us,' said James. 'How about you?'

'Sounds excellent.' Blair looked up at the waiter. 'Two more of the same, please, Louis.' And to James, 'Juliet is coming along in a few minutes; she's phoning the airport to check on her flight tomorrow.'

James said, 'It's settled, then?' and Blair nodded.

'New York for five weeks.' His voice held a certain tenderness as he added, 'Silly girl, she reckons New York is necessary to fertilise some of her new ideas—as if she needed anything to add to what she's already got. But you know what these girls are.' He transferred his smile to Amanda, but the tenderness had gone. This was just social chit-chat, she thought, bringing her into the conversation. Her mind seized gratefully on the fact that Juliet was going to be out of the country—just as if it would make any difference.

That note in Blair's voice when he spoke of Juliet told her all she needed to know.

And when Juliet herself floated across the room to join them a few minutes later, any lingering hope she might have had was finally dispelled. 'James! Lovely to see you. Good trip in Paris?' Her voice was low and slightly husky. 'And this is Amanda? Blair's been telling me.' She smiled in the friendliest way.

The two men had got to their feet and now James resumed his seat while Blair put an arm round Juliet's shoulder. Amanda saw the slight pressure of his fingers. What did that mean? she wondered. Had he been painting a picture of the tiresome little teenager from the back of beyond and was warning Juliet to be discreet? Or did it just mean, 'I love you'? Amanda wasn't sure which was the worst. She smiled back woodenly and could find nothing to say.

'Sit down, my lovely.' Blair pulled out a chair. 'You're to have Lobster Thermidor as a special treat.' His eyes laughed into her wallflower-brown ones and she clapped her hands.

'Super! This can be a double celebration lunch. Celebrating Amanda's arrival and'—she lifted her eyebrows comically—'celebrating getting rid of me for a while!' She slid her arms out of the bolero that fitted over the full, softly-gathered dress she wore. She had probably designed the material herself, thought Amanda, noticing the unusual swirling motifs, the subtle blending of colour—amber and bronze and white—that gave vibrant touches to a background of forest green. Her hair was bronze too, and her skin perfect. She looks like a dryad, thought Amanda, glancing miserably down at her white blouse and grey pleated skirt. And she makes me feel like a fourth-former.

It might have helped a little if she could have disliked Juliet, but as lunch went on she decided that nobody could possibly dislike Juliet. Her vivacity and high spirits seemed

to infect them all. She teased James; sparkled up at Blair,
her long, artistic fingers touching his coat sleeve to emphasize a point; drew Amanda into the conversation, saying
that Devon was one of her favourite places, asking questions, recounting amusing little incidents. No, you couldn't
dislike Juliet, Amanda decided rather wistfully as she
watched Blair's dark eyes narrow with a kind of loving
amusement as he delivered his own brand of mocking re-
partee in response to Juliet's foolery. James had been right.
these two had 'something going for them'. It was the height
of folly to make herself believe anything else.

As the dessert trolley was wheeled up to the table James
said, glancing at his watch, 'We'd better make some plans.
Blair and I have this meeting at three with Pierre Morelle.
Do you want to come along, Juliet?'

She shook her head. 'I've done my part—Blair has the
drawings. I'm just keeping my fingers crossed.'

James nodded. 'We all are.' He looked at Amanda. 'We've
got a big deal in prospect with a French firm and we hope
it's coming up to the boil. That's why I was kept in Paris
the other day.' He glanced at the other two and added,
'Amanda's one of the family now—we must keep her in the
picture; maybe even rope her in to help. What do you say,
Amanda?'

The good food and the wine had bolstered Amanda's
confidence and now she began to feel at ease for the first
time in this company, almost one of them. 'But of course,'
she said with fine seriousness. 'A girl must earn her keep.
Can you use a highly-qualified shorthand-typist?'

James threw up his hands in horror. 'My daughter can't
be a shorthand-typist!'

Amanda turned her clear gaze upon him. 'Amanda Dawson can,' she said serenely.

There was a sudden silence round the table. Then Juliet
clapped her hands and said, 'Up the women!' and Blair
drawled, 'You lost that trick, James,' and James grinned

and said, 'O.K., I get the message. I have an independent young woman on my hands. But at least she's agreed to let me buy her some clothes.' He looked at Juliet. 'If you're not coming to the meeting with us, Juliet, how would it be if you took Amanda shopping? She needs to buy a complete trousseau.'

'Trousseau?' Juliet squeaked the word. 'You're going to be married?'

Blair uttered just one word: 'Trousseau?' He was staring blankly at Amanda, but he looked more than surprised, he looked outraged, as if a trusted friend had betrayed him. She saw again the cold anger she had seen in his face before. Dizzily she thought, He can't *mind*. It couldn't *matter* to him if I were going to be married? and an odd little thrill ran through her.

Then cold reason returned. He was merely peeved because he thought he had been kept in the dark about something she might have been expected to tell him. Amanda's experience of men was limited, but she had already discovered that they can be extremely childish.

She smiled sweetly. 'Married? Oh no, not yet. My father was using the word "trousseau" in a different way.' She looked towards Juliet. 'You see, I'm going to stay with my father for a while and he thought that it would save a journey back to Devon if I had a completely new outfit. It seems horribly extravagant but——'

'——but how absolutely *marvellous*,' Juliet broke in. 'Do let me come with you. I've always thought how splendid it would be to give all my old rags away and start again from scratch.'

So it was arranged. They would split up now and meet again at James's flat at six o'clock. The men went off to their meeting and Amanda found herself in a taxi with Juliet, bubbling with enthusiasm, beside her. 'Harrods, please,' she told the driver. She sat back and twitched her softly-flowing skirt into order. 'Harrods will be best because then we can have everything entered to my account and I can get it back from James later on, and of course they have absolutely *everything*, and plenty of choice. Later on you'll want something really terribly exclusive, and I've a little boutique I can take you to——' She broke off, lifting an eyebrow at Amanda, with a comical grimace. 'Am I being pushy? Do you mind being taken over like this?'

Amanda sank back into her corner of the taxi seat. 'Not a bit,' she said. 'I'm enjoying it.'

Almost unbelievably, that was true. She was actually enjoying being with the girl that Blair was going to marry. It couldn't last, she thought, something would happen to change the pattern; perhaps she would meet another man who would make her forget Blair Craddock.

She could almost hear Gran saying, 'And perhaps pigs might fly!'

Blair slowed the car and glanced at his passenger. 'I think we'll stop for a meal,' he said. 'It'll be lateish when we get back to Radneys and Mrs Fogg hasn't been warned to expect us. That all right with you?'

'Yes, thank you,' said Amanda politely. She fixed her gaze on Blair's strong brown fingers resting on the wheel of his car. There was still enough light to see them by, although the clock on the illuminated dashboard said that it was going on for ten o'clock. A rim of white shirt-sleeve protruded below the dark grey of his suit; a glint of gold from his watch bracelet echoed the wide gold signet ring on his left hand. An engagement ring? Amanda's mood slumped dismally. Her mood had, in fact, been swinging about like a small boat in a heavy sea since they left town, the two of them.

It had been James who suggested that Blair should drive her home. They had all foregathered, as arranged, in James's small flat in St James's, and when the 'shop' talk about the business meeting was over James had said, 'So you see I *have* to stay overnight to finalise the next round of talks in Paris, but I'm not going to be selfish enough to keep Amanda here with me. I'll be busy all morning tomorrow; Juliet will be flying off to New York and Blair says he must turn in to work. So, as you're driving back this evening, Blair, I suggest you take Amanda with you—plus all this paraphernalia.' He smiled tolerantly at the stack of parcels and dress-boxes piled up inside the front door. 'What do you say, Blair? Will you look after my little girl for me?'

'My pleasure,' said Blair formally, but Amanda saw that he was looking at Juliet—she thought with a question in his eyes.

Juliet said, 'I must be off to my hotel to get a good night's sleep before tomorrow.' She smiled at Amanda. 'I suffer awful pangs of jet-lag, and I want to use every possible minute of New York. Goodbye, Amanda, I did enjoy our shopping spree and I'll look forward to seeing you wearing all that lovely gear when I get back.' She leaned forward and kissed Amanda. ' 'Bye, James, and good luck in Paris— I'll be waiting to hear the result.' She turned to Blair and he said quickly,

'I'll see you to your hotel.'

'No—really——'

'I'll see you to your hotel,' he said quietly, and he took her by the arm and led her from the room.

Amanda waited until the door had closed and then turned to her father. 'Couldn't I stay with you?' she said. 'I don't suppose Blair wants to be bothered with me this evening.' Not when he had just said goodbye to the girl he was in love with and wouldn't see again for weeks.

James shook his head very definitely. 'No, I'd rather you went back home,' he said, and for the first time she heard his voice of authority, the quality that had taken him to the top of his particular tree. 'If I could be with you it would be different, but I'll be busy most of tomorrow. And in any case'—he looked humorously around the tiny flat, with the piles of dress boxes and parcels—'you couldn't swing a mouse here, let alone your cottage cat. Also,' he added, 'there's only one bed and I'm much too old and selfish to offer you that and sleep on the floor myself.'

She laughed. James had his own way of getting what he wanted, and he certainly didn't want her to stay in London with him. He seemed almost anxious to get rid of her, which was rather odd in the circumstances, but perhaps she was imagining that. However important the novelty of having a daughter might be to him, his business would be more important. Wasn't his whole life a proof of that?

'Very well, Papa,' she said lightly. 'I'll go with Blair.' It was going to be rather horrid to feel that he was taking her on sufferance, with his head full of Juliet, but there seemed no way out.

'Good girl.' James nodded and slumped into a chair, the weariness back in his face.

'You're tired,' said Amanda quickly. 'Can I get you anything? A drink?'

He grinned at her whimsically. 'What a luxury to be waited upon by a lovely lady! A whisky would be welcome —that cupboard over there.'

She brought him his drink and he tossed it off. 'That's better. Don't worry about me, Amanda, I'm fine. I just let myself get worked up over this French deal—ridiculous, of course, but that's the way I am, I'm afraid. The excitement, the challenge, they mean far more to me than the money involved.'

She nodded thoughtfully. 'I think I can understand a little.' An idea was forming in her mind that she might be able to make herself useful to him, but now wasn't the time to suggest it, so she sat quietly and let him rest while they waited for Blair to return.

Blair had seemed to be a very long time seeing Juliet to her hotel, and Amanda had to be very firm with herself to thrust away the pictures of their leave-taking that insisted upon forming with dismal clarity before her. When he finally got back the two men had found some outstanding business point to talk over, after which all the boxes and parcels had to be carried from the flat to the parking-meter, some hundred yards away, where Blair had left his car. So in the end it had been getting dusk before they left London and they hadn't yet got off the motorway.

Blue countdown markers appeared on the left. Three diagonal lines, then two, then one, and Blair was pulling the car into the service station.

'I don't know if we can get a decent meal here at this time,' he said. 'Would you settle for a snack?'

Being in love was supposed to take your appetite, but Amanda found that she was very hungry. 'I'd love egg and chips,' she said, and chuckled.

'I should think they could produce that.' He opened the car door. 'What's funny about egg and chips?'

'It just struck me that I'm an egg-and-chips girl and you're a Lobster Thermidor man,' she said.

He came round and opened the door on her side and held out his hand. She hesitated, wondering if she could pretend she hadn't seen it. It had been disturbing to sit beside him in the enclosed intimacy of the big car, conscious all the time of the nearness of his firm, hard body; of the chiselled profile that appeared and disappeared in the headlights of approaching cars; even more conscious of the faint masculine smell of him, a blend of cigars and the fine wool of his suit and something tangy that might have been shaving lotion.

He was waiting, hand outstretched. 'Come on, kitten,' he said. 'I'm partial to egg and chips too.' He had been very silent on the drive, but now he sounded deliberately cheerful, as if he had decided to put away sad thoughts of leaving Juliet, and set out to be companionable. She put her hand in his and felt his strong grip for a moment. 'You do like labelling people, don't you, Amanda?' He was mock-serious. 'I've told you before about that—you shouldn't jump to conclusions.'

She pulled her hand away and said crossly, 'I don't, usually. But you can't blame me for making guesses when everybody I meet is a stranger. I have to try and get my bearings.'

He locked the car and tucked his hand under her arm as they made their way between the mass of parked vehicles towards the lights shining out from the restaurant. 'Oh, I don't blame you, my child, I could never blame you for anything,' he said soothingly.

'And don't patronise me either!' she snapped. The touch of his hand through the thin stuff of her summer suit was awakening the overpowering physical response that she was beginning to dread. She wasn't a bad-tempered girl, but at this moment she had an urgent desire to quarrel with him.

But he refused to be drawn. He pushed open the heavy glass door and smiled down at her. 'No, I can see that that would never do,' he said, and she felt much worse than if he had been angry.

The self-service café, with its trimmings of chrome and formica and plastic, was lit whitely, and had a sprinkling of somewhat jaded-looking travellers at the tables. But Amanda was hungry and in no mood to criticise her surroundings, and when she and Blair had pushed their trays along the rail and found an empty table by a window, she sat down to do justice to the plate loaded with egg and chips and the beaker of coffee beside it.

'That was good,' she said at last, and, looking up, found rather to her surprise that Blair's plate was empty too.

'Very good,' he agreed. 'Like something else? More coffee? Pastry?'

'No, thank you.' She expected him to say they would be on their way, but instead he leaned back in his chair and regarded her across the table with that lazy half-smile she was beginning to know off by heart. 'So,' he said, 'you decided to take my advice after all and accept James's invitation to stay.'

She gave him her straight look. 'Well, let's say I decided to stay.'

He grinned. 'All right, so my humble request didn't mean a thing to you. Why should it?'

'I didn't mean it like that. It was just that I didn't really see why you should be so anxious that I should stay.'

'Didn't you?' he said quietly. 'Didn't you really, Amanda?'

Her heart began to race. He didn't mean—he couldn't——? 'No, I didn't,' she said in as ordinary a voice as she could manage.

'I'd have thought it was obvious.' She held her breath, waiting for what he would say next. After a maddening pause, when he selected a thin cheroot from his case and lit it, he continued, 'Well, it obviously meant a lot to James, and so of course it meant a lot to me and the company. We can't get along without your father and he's not been too fit and happy of late. He needed something to perk him up and give him a new interest in life.'

'I see,' she said. What a fool she'd been to hope! And then, because it would be dreadful if he guessed the thoughts that had been passing through her mind, she added more crisply, 'Well, it looks as if I'd made the right choice—for me. I'm getting my reward already—all those lovely clothes that Juliet helped me choose this afternoon. She was super, I don't know what I should have done without her. She seemed to know by instinct just what would suit me. I suppose it's because of her flair for design and colour.' Her voice was coming out commendably firm and light; she felt quite proud of herself. She was confident enough to risk saying, 'You're going to miss her terribly, aren't you? I think she's a wonderful girl.'

She watched his face. He was looking past her, through

the big window to where the car lights flashed past on the motorway, and his expression was serious, almost solemn, as if his feelings were going very deep. Then his eyes came back to her. 'Yes,' he said, 'to both. I *shall* miss her and I *do* think she's a wonderful girl.'

He was smiling straight into her eyes now and she thought, This is my cue. I should say, 'Are you going to marry her?'

But she couldn't say the words, and anyway she knew the answer. She smiled back at him brilliantly—a social smile that seemed to come naturally although she had never needed to use one before to cover up her feelings. 'Well, I think you're jolly lucky to have her,' she said. 'And now, shouldn't we be getting along? I've got all these lovely clothes to unpack and put away when I get back.'

She gathered up her handbag, stood up very slim and straight, and led the way to the door.

CHAPTER FIVE

AMANDA sat on the edge of the swimming pool at Radneys and dangled her feet in the clear, tepid turquoise water. The afternoon sun was warm on her smooth arms and delightfully long legs, which the Devon sun at home had already tanned a pale biscuit colour. She wore a miniscule one-piece swimsuit patterned in navy and white. ('Have that one,' Juliet had advised, 'so much sexier than a bikini. You've got a lovely body, Amanda, you don't want to divide it up into portions.')

For the last two hours she had swum and dived and sunbathed, stretched out on her towel; then swum again. She combed out her hair and let it dry into its natural curves, which hugged her small, well-shaped head and fell in a heavy mass to her shoulders. She looked idly around her, at the swimming pool glittering in the sunlight, the striped loungers in the cedarwood shelter, the small white tables with white, wrought iron chairs and huge gay umbrellas, the sheltering bank of great trees to one side and straight ahead the tops of the stop-netting of the two tennis courts. Behind her, she knew without looking, were the terraced lawns and manicured shrubs, and the beautiful modern house, low and impressive, at the back.

She removed her feet from the water and sat hugging her knees. She might have been suddenly transplanted into some fabulous holiday resort. She sighed. In fabulous holiday resorts—or, at least, in the pictures of them which she had seen—there were always lots of beautiful people. But Amanda was all alone.

Since Blair unloaded her boxes and parcels into her room last night and left her with a friendly but absent, 'See you soon,' she hadn't encountered a soul except Mrs Fogg, who had brought up her breakfast on a tray and served her lunch in the cool, elegant dining room. Elaine hadn't put in an appearance, which was a relief. James would not be home until this evening. There wasn't even a cat or a dog to talk to.

Amanda sighed and wondered how on earth she was going to occupy her time here. She had been busy all her young life—at school, at college, studying, visiting her friends, helping Gran with the shopping, doing her bit towards the usual village fund-raising activities for the church hall, and so on.

What had her father in mind for her? Merely to be here to greet him when he returned from his business affairs? That wouldn't do for her at all and she would have to tell him so. He would have to find a job for her; she had been more than half in earnest when she proposed herself as a secretary. She was sure she could help in some way; she might even be able to take some of the load off him so that —as Gran would say—she would be killing two birds with one stone.

She began slowly to dry her feet, her hair falling forward over her face. She didn't hear footsteps approaching softly over the tiled pool-surround and gave a little jump of surprise when a man's voice, behind her, said, 'Hullo there.'

She squinted up against the sun. 'Hullo,' she said doubtfully. From where she was sitting all she could make out was a pair of long legs in light trousers topped by a pinkish shirt and a rather pale face with reddish hair.

'Sorry, did I startle you?' He dropped down beside her and she saw that he was quite young—late twenties, probably—and had a winning smile and light brown eyes that met her own with frank admiration. 'Christopher French,' he said. 'My mama, who has only just risen from her bed, told me I might find you out here somewhere. So you're Uncle James's long-lost daughter and I'm a sort of step-nephew of his, so we should get acquainted.' He held out his hand.

She put her own hand into it and felt a strong, firm grip. Well, well, she wouldn't have expected the sour and crabby Elaine to produce such a friendly and personable son. 'I hadn't heard about you,' she said.

He put on a rueful expression. 'And I thought my name was a household word! Have you anything very urgent to do at this moment, or shall we exchange our life stories?'

She smiled. 'I'm not quite sure about the life story, but I was just wishing to have someone to talk to, as it happens. I thought even a friendly cat or dog would be preferable to so much of my own company.'

He grinned back at her. 'Wuff, wuff, call me Fido. Seriously though, have they really left you all alone—I call that a crying shame and I shall speak to my mama about it.'

'Oh, please don't,' she said hastily, 'I don't think Mrs French is—well—terribly enthusiastic about my being here. After all, I'm nothing at all to do with her and I certainly wouldn't want to make a nuisance of myself. You see, I've only just arrived really, and I haven't had time to make friends or get to know anybody around here. I expect I shall quite soon. My father will be back at home later on today and then we'll have a talk about what I'm going to do with myself. Just now I'm sort of drifting.'

'Then do let's drift together. I've got a few days' leave; perhaps I could show you round the district? And we could buzz up to Town or over to Bristol if we want to live it up a bit. And, by the way, you don't want to take too much notice of my mama. She gets awfully tetchy when she has one of these migraine things. I'm sure she must have given you the wrong impression; she was telling me just now that she's been living in a sort of daze for the last few days, doped up with tablets just to keep going at all.'

'Oh,' said Amanda, torn between a wish to believe him and a feeling that Mrs French's attitude towards her didn't

New From

Harlequin

the leading publisher
of Romantic Fiction

What secrets lie within the Hotel De La Marine?

For weeks the small French fishing village of Port Royal had been aflame with rumors about the mysterious stranger. Why had he come? What was he after? Challenged by his haughty, yet haunted demeanor, Marie was determined to break through his mask of indifference. But he was as charming as he was cunning, uncanny in perception and driven by vengeance. From the moment she learned his secret, Marie lived with the fear of discovery, and the thrill of danger.

Uncover those secrets with Marie in the gripping pages of *High Wind in Brittany* by *Caroline Gayet*—one of the many best-selling authors of romantic suspense presented by Mystique Books.

MYSTIQUES

Now every month you can be spellbound by 4 exciting Mystique novels like these. You'll be swept away to casinos in Monte Carlo, ski chalets in the Alps, or mysterious ruins in Mexico. You'll experience the excitement of intrigue and the warmth of romance. Mystique novels are all written by internationally acclaimed, best-selling authors of romantic suspense.

Subscribe now! As a member of the Mystiques Subscription plan, you'll receive 4 books each month. Cancel anytime. And still keep your 4 FREE BOOKS!

quite seem to tie in with being in a daze through taking tablets. But she could be wrong and she didn't want to misjudge the woman. 'Oh well, perhaps you're right.'

'I'm sure I'm right,' he said, smiling frankly and sincerely. 'Nobody in their sane senses could be anything but delighted to have you about the place, Amanda.'

'How could you possibly know that? We only met about two minutes ago.'

He looked at her quizzically. 'You're quick off the mark, aren't you—I like that in a girl. But I meant what I said all the same. I've got a sixth sense about people. I find my first impressions always hold good.' He got to his feet, 'Now, what would you like to do? We could swim again if you haven't had enough already. Or how about a game of tennis? There are racquets and balls in the pavilion over there.'

'I'd like that,' said Amanda, 'but I'd have to go in and change.'

'Why? You look super as you are. Pretend you're on holiday at one of the more broadminded resorts where nobody would dream of covering themselves up. Look, I'll join you.' He pulled off his shirt to disclose a well-covered torso. He took her hands and pulled her up. 'Come on, slip on your sandals and let's go.'

As she reached for her rubber-soled sandals she felt her spirits rise. It was nice to have someone to talk to and this young man seemed good fun. He was so open and pleasant —quite a change from Blair, that dark, faintly mysterious character who seemed to have been occupying her thoughts altogether too much for her peace of mind.

The two red shale tennis courts, like everything else at Radney, were perfectly kept and sited, with tall, dark green shrubs behind the stop-netting, and a small wooden pavilion alongside. They procured racquets and balls and Christopher wound up the net. 'Are you very good, because if so you'll have to show me mercy.'

He was being modest, Amanda discovered in the very first game. She was herself of reasonable club standard, but he was much better. As the set went on, though, she found she could lift her game to a standard that surprised herself. It was exhilarating to run in the sunshine with the air warm on her body. She had never played tennis before in anything but the conventional short dress, but this swimsuit gave her quite a remarkable sense of freedom and her limbs seemed to move and swing of their own accord, driving and smashing and serving as never before. In the end she won the set by a narrow margin.

'Good for you!' Christopher came up to the net, grinning and breathing rather hard. 'You're quite a player, aren't you? You see, I have no chauvinist tendencies. I'm quite willing to give the woman best. Want another set?'

'I'm game if you are,' said Amanda, pushing back her hair and laughing. She felt as if she could go on playing for hours. 'Your serve.' She turned to walk back to the base line to receive service.

It was then that she saw him—Blair Craddock, standing leaning nonchalantly against the stop-netting pole. He wasn't smiling.

'Hullo,' she called. 'Lovely day, isn't it?'

From this distance she couldn't hear him reply, if, indeed, he had done so. He looked grimmer than she had seen him look before. She waited a moment, then shrugged and walked across to receive service. For some reason that annoyed her exceedingly her knees felt wobbly.

She didn't score a single point in that game. When she collected the balls for her own service Blair was still standing there, still watching her silently. 'Why can't you go away?' she shouted across to him, laughing a little to show that she wasn't being too serious. 'You're putting me off my game!'

He didn't move or reply but just stood watching her, dark eyes hooded, and all of a sudden she was most embarrassingly aware that her body was scarcely covered at all; she saw her own smooth limbs as he was seeing them and she felt herself flush from her toes right up to her forehead, as if her whole body had caught fire. Then, without a word, he turned and walked away, disappearing behind the bank of dark, evergreen shrubs.

Well, of all the rude—arrogant——! Amanda strode across to the centre line and sent down two services, both of which ended tamely in the bottom of the net.

She didn't win a single game in that set. As she joined Christopher on the seat beside the court she said, 'That was a real anti-climax. Do you want to play the decider?'

He took her racquet and put it with his. 'I wouldn't dream of allowing you to go on, it's much too hot and you must be tired. You certainly weren't doing yourself justice then.' He looked down at her, smiling sympathetically, and she thought: He's standing much closer to me than Blair was and yet I don't feel in the least embarrassed. Christopher was quite definitely masculine and yet he had none of the rather frightening sexual challenge that she found so disturbing about Blair. With a wry, inward grin she thought: Gran would have approved of Christopher.

She said, 'I found a cooler-box in the little chalet by the swimming pool. Shall we go back there and have a lemonade or something?'

He seemed to hesitate for a moment. 'Er—yes, okay.' He looked towards the bushes at the end of the court. 'Wasn't that Blair Craddock I saw just now? Have you met him?'

That was a laugh, she thought grimly. She said, 'Yes, I've met him.'

He nodded. 'Yes, you'd be bound to encounter him. He's your father's partner and a big noise in Caradawc's.' They began to stroll back together along the shrub-lined path to the swimming pool. He glanced down at her. 'How did you get on with him?'

'Oh, quite well,' she said in an offhand voice. 'I've only

met him a couple of times. He seems a very—forceful kind of man.'

Christopher chuckled. 'I said he was a big noise, didn't I? Blair Craddock's a terrific fellow; I only wish I had his brains and his push.' He sounded really admiring.

'You're not connected with the firm yourself?' asked Amanda, wanting to turn the conversation some other way.

'Me? No, not now. I did try it for a while a few years ago, but I got out again fairly quickly. It's not my scene at all, I prefer a quieter life. The rat race doesn't appeal.'

'What do you do, then?'

'I'm in films, on the production side. Nothing so glamorous as acting.' He leaned forward to pull an overhanging branch out of her way. 'I enjoy it, most of the time. I don't exactly make a fortune, but it's interesting and rewarding. Of course, it's different for people like Blair Craddock—he's success-orientated. I've never bothered too much about the money angle myself, it's the quality of life that counts. Poor but happy, that's me.'

They had reached the swimming pool now and Amanda poured cool drinks for them both. When they had drained their glasses she picked up her bathing wrap and Christopher draped it round her shoulders. He tied the cord under her chin and stood back regarding the effect. 'You're a picture, Amanda. You'd look perfect on a screen.' Little laughter lines made creases beside his brown eyes. 'Meeting you here has made my day.' He glanced over his shoulder towards the house and added regretfully, 'But I suppose I'd better be getting along now.'

'You're not staying here with your mother, then?' She was aware of a faint sense of disappointment. She found herself liking this straightforward, rather modest young man. Modesty in a man was quite a change.

He shook his head. 'Unfortunately, no; I'm staying with friends in the next village. You see'—he looked a little awkward—'this isn't my mother's house, and I don't like imposing on your father. I just come up to see her now and again and make sure she's okay. But this time there's been a real bonus. Meeting you—Amanda. I suppose you wouldn't care to have dinner with me?'

'Thank you,' she said, 'I'd like that.'

'Tonight?' he asked eagerly.

'Oh, I couldn't tonight, I'm afraid. My father's coming home.'

He nodded quickly. 'Yes, of course. Tomorrow, then?'

'Well—as far as I know it would be all right. Yes, I'd like to come.'

'Super!' He gripped her hand hard and looked suddenly earnest. 'I'd very much like us to be friends, Amanda. Or am I going too fast?'

She smiled. 'You can't have too many friends.'

It was then that she noticed Mrs French coming towards them across the lawn. She was wearing white today with a good deal of chunky gold jewellery and brown-tinted glasses. Her orange-coloured hair showed darker at the roots as the sunshine caught it.

'Hullo, you two—had a good game?' She seemed to be doing her best to smile and Amanda wished she wouldn't. There was something almost macabre about the gash of scarlet mouth against a face plastered heavily with make-up. 'I see you two have got together. Chris will be company for you, Amanda, I'm afraid I'm not much use to anyone just now. These wretched headaches——'

It would pass for an apology. 'I'm sorry,' said Amanda. 'Aren't you feeling any better today?'

Elaine grimaced. 'Worse, if that's possible. I thought I'd drag myself up and get dressed, but it's no good, I'll have to go back to bed again. Oh, by the way, your father just rang from London, Amanda. He won't be able to get back today and he said to expect him by the early train tomorrow morning. He thought you might like to go along with Fogg to meet him at Bristol. You'd better tell Mrs Fogg what you want her to do about meals.' She cast a haggard look towards her son. 'You'll look after Amanda, then, Chris?'

'You bet,' he said with enthusiasm. 'You don't need to worry about that, Mama. I'd already invited her out to dinner and now that her father's not coming back we'll be able to go. Give me half an hour; I'll just dash back to the Browns' place and make myself pretty'—he grinned facetiously—'and then I'll call back for you, Amanda, and we'll tootle off somewhere in the old flivver. Right?'

She nodded. As things had happened it would have been difficult to refuse, although she had begun to wonder whether Christopher wouldn't turn out to be rather a bore, in his exaggerated eagerness to please. But he surely meant well and she wouldn't hurt his feelings. She smiled at him. 'I'll be ready,' she said, and he pranced off jauntily towards the garage quarters, with instructions to his mother, as an afterthought delivered over his shoulder as he went, to 'have a nice lie-down.'

Elaine watched him go, one hand to her forehead. 'Ah, youth!' she exclaimed dramatically. 'So casual! But he's such a dear, kind boy really.' She turned the dark glasses on Amanda. 'I shall have to give in and go back to bed; I can't struggle on another minute.'

The woman really did look rather ill and Amanda said, 'Is there anything I can do? Do you have a doctor for these attacks?'

'Doctor? Heavens, no! Rest, that's all I need, just rest.'

She went slowly back to the house and through the open patio window. Amanda followed her, watching to see that she didn't trip or fall, for she looked somewhat unsteady. But once inside the large drawing-room her steps became more purposeful and she walked almost buoyantly towards the far end of the room, pausing as she reached the built-in bar. Here she opened the hatch, took down a bottle from the shelf, closed the door again and went out of the room, hugging the bottle against the coat of her white suit.

Amanda stood outside the window, frowning. Then she shrugged. Ah well, if Elaine French found that alcohol was a cure for a headache, who was she to be suspicious? The woman had certainly seemed more inclined to be less hostile towards her, and that was a relief.

She was aware that someone had come up behind her and turned to see Blair Craddock standing there. In the greenish light that filtered through the frosted glass roof of the canopy above the patio he looked at his most saturnine. Amanda's heart began to thump so hard that she was almost sure he must hear it.

She heard herself give a little gasp and pulled the bathing wrap closer. 'You gave me a fright—I didn't hear you.'

The thick dark lashes shadowed his eyes. 'If I wanted to make your heart beat faster I could think of a better way than creeping up on you unawares.'

She could feel the blood in her cheeks. Beast, she thought, he knows perfectly well the effect he has on me. He probably thinks it's funny—the soppy teenager with a crush. There must have been plenty of them; he must have all the little typists in his office yearning after him.

'As a matter of fact,' he was saying, 'I was looking for you. I've just been talking to your father on the phone and it seems he can't get back tonight. He suggested that I should take you out to dinner.'

'I shouldn't dream of imposing on your kindness,' she said loftily, and then wished she hadn't because it sounded so juvenile.

He grinned easily. 'Come off it, Amanda. You know I didn't mean it like that. I should enjoy taking you out.'

'Really? Then I'm sorry to have to disappoint you. As a matter of fact I already have a dinner engagement.'

He went very still. 'Not with Christopher French, I hope?'

'I don't see that it's your business, but if you must know, yes, I have accepted his invitation.'

Blair's mouth was a straight line. 'Then you'll have to tell him that you have a prior engagement. With me.'

'*Have* to?' She turned her level blue-grey gaze on him.

'Yes, have to. I'm sorry if I sound peremptory, but there's no other way of putting it.'

Normally Amanda was a peaceable girl, but there was something inside her that reacted just like a switch being snapped when anyone tried to dominate her. The switch worked now; Amanda went over to automatic pilot. She seemed to grow in years, in confidence, in dignity. 'And why,' she said very quietly, 'should you imagine that I would take orders from you, Mr Craddock?'

He took his hands out of his pockets, his eyes studying her face. 'The orders, as you call them, don't issue from me, they issue from your father. When I told him that Christopher French had put in an appearance here in his absence, he nearly had a fit. His words were something like, "Keep that objectionable little two-timer away from my daughter." That's a paraphrase, of course, his language was much more colourful than that, but I'll spare your youthful ears. I had to calm him down—it's bad for him to get so worked up.'

'So,' said Amanda slowly, 'it wasn't just Mr Blair Craddock thinking he could dictate to me, it was a directive from head office. Well, I may as well tell you, and I'll tell my father when I see him, that I don't take orders from anybody. I'm over eighteen and no one has the right to run my life for me. If I want to go out with Christopher French, I shall do.'

His eyes narrowed to dark slits. 'You won't, you know,' he said softly.

'And who's going to stop me? Do you intend to do it by force?'

His eyes travelled over her and she was hotly aware that her bathing wrap had fallen open, but some new pride stopped her from clutching it round her to hide the near-nakedness beneath from his suddenly appreciative gaze.

'Since you suggest it, that might be quite an idea,' he said, drawling out the words. 'But I don't think it will be necessary.'

Amanda suddenly lost her cool. 'Oh,' she blurted out, 'I think you're unbearable! I'm going in to change for dinner —with Christopher.'

It wasn't until she had reached her bedroom and was sitting on the bed, still trembling from the encounter, that it occurred to her that she had not found out why Christopher should be considered such an unsuitable companion for her. All she had been concerned with was winning a sort of fight with Blair.

It seemed so unfair that her father—and probably Blair also—should be so prejudiced against Christopher, when he had spoken with such admiration of them and of Caradawcs. It was simply because he was the artistic type, she explained to herself, the sort of young man who would be despised by rich and successful men of business. He had probably made a thorough mess of the job he had held in the firm for a short time, and her father was still holding it against him.

It really wasn't fair, she thought, and if her father imagined that he could choose her friends, just because she had agreed to stay here with him for a few months, then he would have to revise his ideas. And if Blair Craddock tried to use his arrogant and high-handed methods to make her do what he told her, just as if she were really the schoolgirl she had been such a short time ago, then *he* had a surprise coming to him! She would wear one of her pretty new dresses, and she would go out with Christopher, and she would make up her own mind about him, she decided, bubbling with indignation.

She got up and gave the wardrobe door an impatient shove and it glided back smoothly to disclose a rail of delightful clothes. If she had been going out with Blair, she thought, working up her resentment into a fine fury, she would have chosen that black and white one, the most sophisticated of the lot, just to show him she wasn't a child to be bullied and ordered about. But there was no need to prove anything to Christopher, she told herself comfortably; he accepted her as a grown-up and an equal, which did a lot for her confidence.

She chose a pretty, romantic dress of subtle blue, patterned in dusky pink and violet, laid it on the bed and went into the adjoining bathroom.

She continued to think about Blair, fuming, while she showered and put on her make-up. Half an hour, Christopher had said. She would wait just that long and then go down to meet him. Surely, by then, Blair would have taken himself away; he couldn't be so brash as to confront Christopher in her presence and make a scene.

But she wasn't sure. She wasn't sure of anything about Blair Craddock, the man who always seemed to be lurking in the background. It had been amusing and intriguing just at first but now the humour had gone out of the situation. She had to admit that the man seemed to have a devastating physical appeal for her that was quite new. When her friends at college discussed the men who 'turned them on' she had wondered just what they meant. Well, now she knew. But he wasn't the only man in the world, she assured herself. There would be other men who would be just as disturbing, just as exciting. Men who would treat her like a grown-up and an equal. Like Christopher, for instance. Perhaps if she let him kiss her tonight then——

She sighed as the mirror gave her a reflection of Blair's olive-green dressing gown hanging over the back of a chair in a corner of the room. Who, she thought bleakly, was she trying to convince?

She put on the dress and cheered up a little. Juliet had loved this dress and Amanda had to admit that it did something for her. The colour made her eyes bluer, the whites very clear; the drawstring gave her waist a fragile look and pleasantly accentuated the swelling curve of her breast. Yes, it was just the dress for a summer evening. She brushed her shining hair and glanced at her watch. Just over half an hour had passed. 'Well, here goes,' she said aloud, and found that, ridiculously, she was trembling as she picked up the matching stole and the small white kid handbag.

She ran softly down the corridor. Christopher hadn't said where he would meet her. Above all she wanted to avoid Blair, if he were still anywhere about. So she turned away from the front door, went through the garden room and out on to the lawn at the side of the house. From here she made her way stealthily towards the front drive, trying not to look at the wing of the house where Blair had his quarters. How absurd, just as if she were a Victorian miss stealing out to a secret assignation with an admirer. She quickened her pace.

Then, with a sinking feeling of inevitability, she saw Blair emerge from the house just as a red sports car rounded the corner of the drive and drew up on the far side of the forecourt. He must have been keeping a watch on her— spying, she thought in disgust. He too had changed—into a lightweight, silver-grey suit which fitted closely across his wide shoulders and made him look tough and muscular—a very formidable man indeed.

Christopher had seen her now and he lifted a hand and went to open the car door; then he saw Blair approaching and shut it again with a slam. Amanda came to a halt about ten feet away and heard Blair say in a voice that crackled with ice, 'You know bloody well you're not welcome here, French. I suggest you remove yourself straight away.'

Amanda stared as if she were watching a play. Surely no man would allow himself to be spoken to like that and re-main sitting down? But to her amazement that was just what Christopher French did. He sat very still, one arm resting along the car door, looking up at Blair, who seemed to tower above him.

'I suppose I can come here to visit my mother,' he said

rather loudly. His pale face under the reddish hair had turned even paler and there was a hectic spot of colour on each cheekbone.

Blair put both hands in his pockets slowly. 'Possibly.' His voice was dangerously quiet. 'But you're not here to visit your mother, are you? You're here under the entirely mistaken impression that you're taking Amanda out.'

The other man began to bluster. 'And why the hell not—she promised——'

'A mistake,' said Blair smoothly. 'She must have forgotten she had a prior date with me. Now push off, Chris, while the going's good.' There was a hard contempt in his voice as he added, 'It was a pretty forlorn hope, anyway, wasn't it?'

The two men glared at each other and suddenly Christopher seemed to shrink before Amanda's eyes. He sat there for a moment or two, saying nothing, then he glanced over towards her with a little shrug. 'Sorry, sweetheart, but you see how it is? Another time, perhaps.' He smiled feebly.

Then, while Amanda still stood amazed, he started the engine, swung the car around and drove off down the drive.

She watched the car until it was out of sight and then, her cheeks pink and her eyes stormy, she glared at Blair, turned on her heel and marched back towards the house. He was beside her in a moment, his hand clamped on to her wrist, stopping her in her tracks.

'You have a dinner date,' he said. 'Remember?'

'Not with you I haven't,' she shot at him furiously. 'I never in my life saw such a disgusting exhibition of bad manners!'

'Oh, I wouldn't put it as strongly as that.' He was still holding her wrist. 'I merely got rid of a most unacceptable visitor. He didn't need much persuading, as you may have noticed. Some of the others may not be so easy to deal with.'

'Others? I don't know what you're talking about. What others?'

He smiled his dark-lashed smile. How could she ever have found it so attractive? Just at the moment she wanted to hit him—hard. 'There'll be plenty of others,' he drawled. 'You're not a little typist now, you know. You're a rich man's daughter. Your market value has gone up considerably.'

He was holding her left wrist. Her right hand came up, but he caught it before it could make contact. Turning her towards him he laughed down into her infuriated face. 'Ah-ah, temper!' he murmured. He looked as if he were enjoying this encounter considerably.

'Let me go!' she breathed, wrenching ineffectively at her prisoned hands. 'I think you're disgusting—cynical—horrible——'

'Yes, I am horrible. And cynical. It's pleasant to agree on something, don't you think? Now, suppose the kitten sheaths her claws and we'll drive over and have a meal together. You won't get much here; the Foggs have just gone out for the evening. I told Mrs Fogg you were dining with me.'

She pursed her lips obstinately. 'I'm not coming. I'll make a meal for myself.'

'Then you'll have to make one for me too,' he said placidly. 'I promised your father to keep an eye on you until he comes back.'

She stamped her foot. 'Good heavens! Anyone would think I was a bit of priceless porcelain, to be kept in a glass case.'

He grinned. 'You're much more valuable than that to James. And much prettier than any Minton shepherdess. That's a very attractive dress; did Juliet choose it for you?'

'Yes,' she said shortly.

She pulled away from him and he released one wrist but kept hold of the other, encircling her waist with his free hand. She started to move towards the house again. Being so close to him was a painful pleasure and if they got inside he would *have* to let her go.

'I'm sure you're a great little cook,' said Blair, 'but wouldn't it be rather a bore to have to get a meal? Wouldn't it be much easier to drive out to Shevely—seeing that you're saddled with me in any case? Then I could explain how and why I disposed of Christopher French so easily.'

They walked up the steps and through the patio door into the drawing room. Amanda stopped.

Blair lifted his eyes to the ceiling. 'They do a very nice line in scampi at the Shevely Arms,' he reflected. 'Great—fat—golden—luscious—scampi!'

Scampi! Amanda could see them, almost smell them. She realised that she was very hungry. And suddenly she could hear Gran's voice saying, 'Don't cut off your nose to spite your face.'

Blair had promised to explain, she argued briefly with herself, and perhaps it was only fair to give him the chance.

Christopher French really had been absolutely feeble.

Amanda began to smile. 'All right,' she said. 'I'll come.'

Hours later Blair's big, sleek car cruised gently back towards Radneys in the dusk of the summer evening. Amanda snuggled into the corner of the passenger seat and sniffed the dew-damp hedgerow scents that came in through the open window. She might have been back at home; but she had never driven in a car like this in Devon, nor with a man like Blair Craddock beside her at the wheel.

She reflected with a faintly guilty feeling that if she had been given the choice, at this moment, of staying where she was or of being transported back to King's Holton, she would have chosen to stay. Just for the time being she could manage to forget that Blair considered her a child; she could even blot out the thought that he was in love with Juliet. It was enough to have the bliss of sitting beside him and driving in cushioned ease along the country lanes, with the moon just coming up among the trees.

She was beginning to know the road now. Just before the turning off to Radneys he drew the car on to the wide grass verge and switched off the engine. He turned to her, his arm resting along the back of the front seat. Now, she supposed, he would give her the facts about his treatment of Christopher.

It had been Blair who had suggested that they postpone explanations until after dinner and Amanda had agreed. To tell the truth, she had almost forgotten about the incident as she sat opposite Blair at a window table in the small, quiet, dining room of the Shevely Arms, enjoying scampi and *pommes frites* and *petits pois*, accompanied by a sparkling wine whose name she didn't catch, except that it was something very long and in a language that sounded like German.

They had talked about their mutual likes and dislikes—in food, in books, in music, and discovered that they shared a number of special delights. It had been, Amanda thought dreamily, rather like a very first date—only no first date had ever held such magic for her.

But now, evidently, reality was going to intrude.

He took his time about speaking, and his words were a surprise. 'Still hating me, Amanda?' he said in his quizzical voice.

She looked over at him, startled. The moonlight threw shadows across his face and the silver-grey of his coat, emphasizing the blackness of his hair and the winged, slanting eyebrows. He looked like Harlequin, she thought rather dizzily. Or Mephistopheles!

'Hate you?' She kept her voice light. 'Why should I?'

She saw his half-smile. 'I seem to remember that not so very long ago you were flashing around words like disgusting and cynical and horrible in connection with the way I disposed of your new friend Christopher French.'

She pushed aside the thought that it really didn't matter any longer. She nearly said as much to him. Then, in case he guessed the reason for her sudden lack of interest, she said, 'You *were* rather beastly to him.'

'Yes,' he agreed, sounding satisfied.

There was a silence. Then he said, 'I suppose you found him a straightforward type?'

'As it happens, I did.'

'Frank? Cheerful? Open? Charming?'

'I don't know what you're getting at,' said Amanda, 'but yes, if you like. All those things.'

'H'm. Then I rather wish I'd been even beastlier to him.'

She moved her shoulders impatiently and sat staring ahead through the windscreen. 'I can see you don't intend to tell me anything at all. All that business about explanations was just a—a smokescreen to try and put me off.'

Out of the corner of her eye she saw him shake his head slowly. 'No, not a bit of it. The fact of the matter is that it's your father's house and your father has already told Christopher French in no uncertain terms to keep away from it. If you want chapter and verse of the reasons, my girl, you'll have to ask James. That's all you're getting from me. You do see, don't you, that it's not up to me to tell you.'

'Ye-es, I suppose so.'

He moved quickly, leaning close to peer into her face. 'My God, Amanda, don't tell me you've fallen for that rotten little——' he checked himself. 'Tell me you didn't.'

'No, of course I didn't,' she said quite crossly. 'It was just that——'

'Yes?'

'If you must know, he made me feel like a grown-up.' She twisted her hands together on her lap. 'Everyone else in this place makes me feel like a schoolgirl.'

There was a long, long silence. At last Blair said, 'Yes. Yes, I see.' He nodded his head slowly several times. 'There doesn't seem to be any answer to that one. We'll just have to see what we can do about it.'

He started the car again and they drove in silence back to Radneys.

The low, sleek house lay silent among the trees, with only a few diffused lights showing inside its several wings. Blair opened the door that led to his own apartment. 'Can I persuade you to stay for a while? A drink—or some more coffee?'

'No, thank you,' she said. He didn't really want her company; he was sorry for her, that was all, and he was carrying out her father's wishes. Perhaps he even had a passing thought that by inviting her into a man's rooms at night he was doing something for her pathetic lack of confidence, making her feel more worldly and sophisticated.

'I'd like to go to my own room,' she said. 'Don't bother, I know my way now.'

He ignored that and put his hand at her elbow as they walked down the corridors and across the lobby. Reaching her bedroom she pushed open the door, and the first thing she saw was Blair's olive-green dressing gown hanging over the back of a chair. 'Oh, your dressing gown,' she said, 'I meant to return it to you.' She went into the room and took it from the chair. 'Thank you for lending it to me.'

Standing in the doorway he took it from her, saying nothing, and suddenly Amanda's heart began to throb and her throat went dry. She knew they were both remembering that other evening when he had—had——

'Well, thank you for the evening, and the meal. The scampi was delicious,' she croaked hurriedly. That sounded the kind of speech one made to a kind uncle. Oh, well—— She smiled up at him, half-apologetically, and turned into the room, her hand groping for the light switch.

His own hand covered hers before she could find the switch, moved up her arm to her shoulder and his touch was hard and warm through her thin dress, sending a convulsive shiver all through her. Quite slowly he turned her round to face him. His back was towards the corridor, his face in shadow, but she could see the gleam in dark, liquid eyes.

He said softly, 'I warned you not to smile at me like that, you know.' And he drew her close, unresisting, crushing her slim body against his with a kind of deliberate strength. His kiss was just as deliberate—his mouth firm against hers. But Amanda was in no mood to analyse a kiss. She was in his arms and she was lost in delight. Her mouth clung to his; her arms went up round his neck, her fingers winding into the dark hair. It was a kind of madness, but she was beyond caring. The empty, dimly-lit corridor disappeared and there was nothing but their two bodies, locked together in an embrace that she wanted never to end.

Then she realised that, very gently, he was disengaging himself, holding her away from him. 'Thank you, Amanda,' he said, 'that was very sweet.' And he added quietly, 'I don't think of you as a schoolgirl, you know.' He held her a moment longer, smiling down at her, cool, controlled. Then he said quietly, 'Goodnight, Amanda. Sleep well.' And he walked away from her down the long corridor.

She went into the room and stood beside the bed, fighting back her tears. He had meant it kindly, she told herself, he was sorry for her—just a naïve schoolgirl, feeling a little lost in unfamiliar, sophisticated surroundings. Not in his league at all, of course, but he was prepared to amuse her, while her father was away, as one might amuse a lonely, lost child.

She walked across to the window and drew back the curtains, which had been closed. Mrs Fogg must have come in, she thought absently, and wondered if she had been anywhere about to witness that little episode. She stared out of the window at the moonlit garden outside. Radneys looked different in the moonlight—more mellow perhaps—with its lawns and shrubs and flower-beds. It was really very beautiful; she might even grow to like and accept it if things were different. From here she could see the tall uprights that held the stop-netting round the tennis courts—where Blair had stood and watched her playing this afternoon, and then walked away without a word. He must have thought she was a silly little girl—showing off and flirting in her scanty swimsuit.

She grasped the edges of the curtains in both hands, her head bent, the hot tears scalding her eyes. 'I can't stay here,' she said aloud. 'I can't—I'll have to tell James that it's no good.'

Across the room the bedside telephone buzzed. She sped across the room and picked it up. Who could it be but Blair, on the house telephone?

'Miss Dawson, this is Mrs Fogg,' came that lady's crisp, sensible tones, and Amanda sank down on to the bed, breathing rather quickly. 'I thought you might have come in. Your father's on the line from London, miss, and he'd like to speak to you.'

'Amanda, my dear,' came her father's voice. 'So very sorry I couldn't get back today. Mrs Fogg tells me that Blair has been entertaining you. That's splendid. I was afraid you might——' he seemed to hesitate '—might have been on your own. Now listen, pet, have you been to Paris?'

'Paris?' she said, her voice a little muffled. 'I was there on my last school holiday—on an exchange thing, staying with some people in Aulnay-sous-Bois. We visited Paris several times. It was super.'

'Good. Splendid. Then your passport will be okay. I've got to fly over again tomorrow and I want you to come with me. Fogg will drive you up here in the morning and we can catch an afternoon plane. Just pack a few things, you'll know what to bring——'

'Tomorrow?' breathed Amanda. 'But I can't——' In her league people didn't just fly off to Paris at a moment's notice. They planned and booked and talked it over for weeks and——

Dazedly, she realised that James hadn't stopped speaking. 'We'll have a good time, Amanda. My business will only take an hour or two and then we can go around and see the sights—a show—dinner—I'm looking forward to it. Okay with you, my dear?'

'Okay,' she said weakly. 'You've taken my breath away, rather. But—but it will be lovely.'

'Splendid! Have an early night and I'll look out for you tomorrow.' His enthusiasm and affection came right across the wire to her and when she had said goodbye and replaced the receiver she sat looking at it, thinking that she had been selfish and foolish to think of leaving. Anyway, she had promised.

And at least, in Paris, she would be a long way from Blair.

CHAPTER SIX

TRAVELLING with James was very different from travelling with a school party, Amanda mused, as the Paris plane became airborne the following afternoon. As she released her seat-belt she turned to look at him, sitting beside her. He had taken off his coat and in his white shirt with a pattern of thin brown stripes, his brown silk tie, gold cuff-links, neatly-brushed hair and close-shaven cheeks, he looked exactly what he was—a top executive, an important man in the country's industry, a first-class traveller through life. But the monkey-eyes were tired and there were deep furrows in his brow, and again she felt a pull of affection for this father whom she scarcely knew. You would have to take James on his own terms, but there was something in her that responded to him. Whether she wanted it or not, she was involved in his life.

Because of that feeling she had to get things straight from the start. She said, 'I'm thrilled to be coming to Paris and I'm sure it's going to be wonderful, but—but may I ask you something, and get it out of the way before we get there?'

'Of course—anything,' James smiled at her.

'Did you—was it because Blair told you that Christopher French had come to Radneys that you invited me to come with you to Paris?'

The smile disappeared and his mouth became grim. 'I can see that you're a girl who likes the truth, so I may as well admit it—it *was* partly because of that, but only partly. I wanted you with me; I was missing you. And the news that French had had the nerve to come back and was hanging around you made up my mind for me.'

When she didn't reply he leaned over and covered her

hand with his. 'Please believe that I don't want to play the heavy father, and lay down the law. But you've led a quiet life up to now, haven't you, and this world of mine will have its pitfalls for you, until you begin to find your way around in it. I must say that when I heard that French was practising his charms on you it shook me, I can tell you.'

She said, with a show of spirit, 'I can look after myself, you know. I'm not a child.'

He didn't pretend to misunderstand. 'I wasn't really thinking of your virtue, my dear,' he said drily. 'It wouldn't have suited Christopher's book to take that line with you. No, I was thinking of something much more devious and in line with his character. If he could have succeeded in making you fall in love with him, what could I have done? Fathers can't lock their daughters away in their bedrooms these days, to protect them from unwise romances.'

'But I wouldn't——' she began, and stopped. She could hardly say, I wouldn't have fallen in love with him because I've been idiotic enough to fall in love with Blair Craddock, could she?

He was regarding her speculatively. 'What did you think of him—honestly?'

'I liked him.'

'Yes,' said James. 'So did we all—at first, when he joined the firm. He was Deirdre's—my wife's—nephew, why should we have doubted him? He came to Radneys constantly—made himself one of the family. He was in my own department, he knew everything that was going on. And for a long time he deliberately and systematically cheated. Never mind the details—you'll have to take my word for it —he let me down personally and he put in jeopardy the good name of the firm. That was quite enough for me.' His voice was bitter.

Amanda said nothing. She had liked Christopher—she admitted it—but certainly not enough to fight his cause, even if it had seemed possible and in the light of the plain, hard facts that James had just recounted, it didn't seem possible.

Her father was watching her closely. 'You *do* understand, my dear?'

'I think so,' she said quietly. 'But don't let's talk about it any more. Let's talk about Paris—tell me what this important deal is all about. Will you?—I'd like to know.'

James looked doubtful. 'Do you really want to?' He flicked through the sheaf of papers he had brought out of his briefcase.

'You're not going to say, "The little woman mustn't bother her pretty head with all this dry old stuff," I hope?'

He chuckled. 'I hope I know better than to take that line with an educated young woman of today!'

'Well then,' she said eagerly, 'try me. I did have a business training, you know. I might be able to be useful to you. Could you use an assistant?'

A slow grin spread over his tired face. 'Could I? You know, I believe you're a chip off the old block, as they say.'

'I believe I might be,' she smiled.

James was beaming now. 'It's an idea. It's a great idea, if you'd like to try it. We'd expand our team to four—you and I and Blair and Juliet.'

Blair and Juliet! It always seemed to come back to that.

Amanda straightened the jacket of her cream travelling suit. 'How long has Juliet been with the firm?' she asked conversationally.

'Not very long—about a year, I'd say. Blair met her again in London—he'd known her before, apparently—and she was looking for a permanent job. He offered her one and she jumped at it and from then, we've never looked back. It was a lucky break. She's a wonderful girl, didn't you think?'

'Yes,' said Amanda evenly. 'I liked her very much.' She bent her head over the sheaf of papers. 'Now, give the new

girl her first lesson and see how much her business training is worth.'

By the time the plane came in to land Amanda knew a
great deal more about the business side of Caradawcs than
she had thought possible—and found it fascinating. 'This
new French deal is really important, then, isn't it?' she
said, and her eyes were shining.

James stacked the papers away in his briefcase. 'The
most important thing that's happened since I teamed up
with John Craddock—Blair's father. We started to modern-
ise and expand a bit then. Caradawcs had always been in
the high price range and we meant to keep it that way, but
it was slow going. But after a while we took off and we're
now in the top of the home market and well established in
the States. The French agency means more than just
France—it means the whole of the E.E.C., of course. Big
stuff!'

'And it's all going to be tied up tomorrow morning?'

'I can't see anything to stop it. They just needed this
one more set of figures'—he patted the briefcase—'and
that's it.'

She said, 'I'll wait for you and keep my fingers crossed.'

'Wait for me? Certainly not! I shall take you along with
me and introduce you as my second-in-command. The
sooner you begin to meet people and get into the run of
things the better.'

A voice over the intercom announced that they would be
coming in to land in five minutes. James smiled down at
Amanda and squeezed her hand very hard. 'I feel,' he said
seriously, 'as if I'd come in to land already.'

And she couldn't think, then, why his choice of words
should have sounded to her so strangely ominous.

Amanda sat before the mirror in her luxurious Paris hotel
room the following evening and the events of the past
twenty-four hours passed in front of her eyes like a brilliantly coloured film strip.

Paris, with her father, was a different Paris from the one she had visited as a schoolgirl, accompanied by the homely French family she had been staying with. She had loved it then, but now it was pure magic with its wide, tree-lined boulevards, its gardens and parks, and the restaurants with little tables and chairs on the pavement, under their bright canopies. Last night, after they had dined, they had wandered out into the warm June evening and sat for hours at one of these tables and sipped coffee and watched darkness fall over the city with its glitter of lights and soft swish of cars and fussy pip-pipping of taxis, and the scent of flowers from some street stall out of sight.

They had talked and talked. Amanda felt now that they had begun to make up the years of separation, and come close to establishing a warm and loving relationship. Gran had been a darling, but having a father like James was a vastly more stimulating experience, and in spite of her earlier doubts and worries, she found herself beginning to take to this new life like the proverbial duck to water.

This morning she had gone with James to the offices of his French business colleagues. She had worn the cream suit of heavy silky material and pinned on to the lapel the large piece of costume jewellery that James had bought for her in the Boulevard Haussman—a spectacular brooch of twisted gilt filigree set with amber. With the suit she had teamed brown patent shoes with high heels and narrow ankle straps, and a matching handbag. She felt that she looked good, and when she walked into the impressive office of the French firm beside James she saw the men eye her with evident pleasure and approval as her father introduced her as his daughter and new personal assistant.

She sat in on their meeting and listened to everything. Her father spoke good French and the meeting was conducted in that language. Amanda had taken French at 'A' level at school and continued with commercial French in her secretarial course, so she was able to follow most of the words although she didn't, naturally, understand the finer points of the deal they were concluding. But the men gave her a pleasant sense of being included, looking in her direction and once or twice addressing her personally. It was heady and stimulating stuff, to be transported from a provincial secretarial college to the board room of a top international firm, and she found herself responding to the occasion with a kind of elation. Her cheeks had a pretty flush and her eyes sparkled like the sunlight on the river which could be glimpsed through the office window. If young Mr Raikes, from the solicitor's office in Exeter, could have seen her at that moment he would have been confirmed in his guess that Amanda had star quality.

When they finally left the offices of the company, with an arrangement to dine together that evening to cement the new deal, Amanda felt that she was on the threshold of a new and vitally interesting life.

'You knocked 'em for six, my darling,' James chuckled as they left the office and walked towards the Champs Elysées. 'Frenchmen, it seems, have no objection to women being intelligent as well as beautiful. Pierre couldn't take his eyes off you—just as well that he's bringing his wife this evening. Even so, I shall give myself the pleasure of buying you a new dress to wear. It's an occasion to celebrate—the signing of the contract, and our first time in Paris together.'

There had followed a lovely long afternoon of feminine pleasure. James, saying that he would rest at the hotel, escorted her to an elegant establishment off the Rue La Fayette and left her in the care of a woman who looked to Amanda more like her idea of one of the French aristocracy than a vendeuse. But Madame Savin had proved cordial and helpful, and enthused in a stately fashion over Amanda's figure, hair, complexion. After an hour or more spent choosing a dress in the perfumed salon with its plushy carpet and little gold chairs, Amanda was escorted to the beauty salon, presided over by a swarthy young man who, after going into raptures over her hair and her skin, proceeded to advise her about the absolute necessity of improving both out of all recognition, which made Amanda smile to herself.

'I leave it to you entirely,' she told him sweetly, and while she was swathed in towels and lowered back to feel the cool water trickling over her head she could hear Gran say, 'In for a penny, in for a pound.'

But now, hours later, as she sat in her hotel room studying the result, she had to admit that the swarthy young man had been right. She hardly recognised herself as the pretty, fresh, ingenuous young country girl who had arrived at Radneys and been bowled over by the modern sophistication of the establishment and the people in it. Now, swept along by circumstances, she looked part of that sophistication.

Her hair had been dressed in an elegant, curly chignon and shone intriguingly with every movement of her small head. She ran her fingers over it now, as the young Frenchman had done with a kind of sensuous enjoyment, and watched it bounce back as he had promised. '*Charmante—délicieuse*——' he had murmured, his eyes meeting hers in the mirror, and she hadn't been quite sure whether he was referring to the hair-style exclusively.

Her face looked different, too, with its silky, translucent, youthful make-up. 'It will remain all evening—just so——' the young woman in the beauty salon had assured her, adding the final touch of pearly colour which made Amanda's clear blue-grey eyes look enormous in her small, delicate face. 'The eyes are the best feature for Mademoiselle—they require the accent *très subtil*—so!' She stood back and regarded her handiwork with satisfaction.

Now, regarding herself in the mirror, Amanda felt a similar satisfaction. Why deny it?—it was wonderful to be young in Paris in June. Paris, the city of romance! Just for a moment the image of Blair Craddock came before her eyes, as clearly as if he had been looking over her shoulder in the mirror. It was uncanny how vivid it was. She saw the glint in sleepy, dark eyes; the pull of muscles beside his mouth; the flash of teeth against deeply-tanned cheeks. For a moment she almost felt the touch of his hand on the softness of her bare shoulder, and felt a long shiver pass through her.

She stood up abruptly. Stop it, she told herself. Stop it this minute. You're here to get your attitude to Blair Craddock sorted out in your mind, not to moon over him. She took the lace blouse and dark blue skirt that she had finally chosen to wear for the dinner this evening down from its hanger and stepped into it. The silk underslip glided over her body with a coolness that shocked her into something like sanity. Reaching over to pull up the zip she said aloud, 'He's the man in the background—remember? And that's where he's going to stay, from now on.'

She wasn't the inexperienced little teenager she had been only a few days ago. She was Miss Amanda Dawson, the daughter of James Dawson, a director of a top firm of textile makers. She had the promise of being a member of that same firm. That made Blair merely a colleague in the firm. And Juliet too. It was going to take a bit of getting used to, but her confidence was increasing all the time, and she would make new friends—men friends, too—and sooner or later she would wake up one day and find that this crazy passion for Blair Craddock had passed—with the man himself—into the background of her life. It would end up just where it started, she assured herself.

There was a tap on the door and her father peeped in. 'Permission to enter? Sorry I wasn't around when you got back. I had some telephoning to do and then I must confess I fell fast asleep. Must have been the result of all the excitement this morning.' He came further into the room, his eyes losing their tiredness as they took in the figure of Amanda in her new dress. 'My word! You *have* used the afternoon to advantage, my child.' He took both her hands and held her away from him as he examined her from head to foot. 'You look'—he shook his head helplessly, smiling—'the only term I can think of is the overworked one "out of this world". But on this occasion it really does apply.'

Amanda dimpled. 'I'm glad you like me. I'm afraid I've cost you an awful lot of money.'

'I can afford it,' said James. He sat down rather heavily in one of the small chairs. 'And that dress is worth every franc, however many it cost. It's absolutely right for you.'

She turned back to the mirror. It would have been possible to say, now, making a joke of it, 'Rather a difference from the last party dress you saw me in!' He had been angry about that whole episode; furious with Elaine for dressing her up like that. He had never mentioned the matter since and Amanda would have liked to ask him about Elaine; to find out if he really had any intention of marrying her or if that was merely wishful thinking on Elaine's part. Life at Radneys would be simpler if she knew exactly what Elaine's position was.

But through the mirror she saw her father's face. It was alarmingly sallow and there were great dark rings beneath the sad monkey-eyes. She turned quickly and went over to him. 'Are you all right, James? You look rather weary.' She put a hand gently on his shoulder. 'Do you feel up to this celebration dinner—*really*? We could put it off.' Her eyes were anxious.

He drew in a breath and grinned up at her. 'I'm fine, you mustn't bother about me.' He pulled himself to his feet. 'We'll go down, if you're ready, and have a drink before the others arrive, shall we? Oh, and by the way, I was on the phone to Blair earlier on, to let him know that everything was signed and sealed. He's going to try to hop over and join us this evening if he can make it. He wasn't quite sure when I spoke to him. It would be good to have him at the party with us, don't you think?'

Amanda's heart began to race uncomfortably. It was too bad, she told herself, that she couldn't get away from Blair, even here in Paris; it made her determined resolve to think of him as merely a colleague into an even more difficult task. But she couldn't stop the quiver of excitement that ran through her at the prospect of seeing him again tonight; and the reflection that her mirror gave back to her added an innocent pleasure. Surely, seeing her as she was tonight, dressed and groomed as a Parisienne, he could no longer treat her as the naïve teenager she had proved to be on their first disastrous meeting.

Her father was looking rather hard at her. 'You would like to have Blair with us, wouldn't you, Amanda?'

She felt her cheeks go suddenly hot and turned away quickly, to pick up her evening bag and short white velvet cape. 'Oh yes, of course,' she said in a throw-away tone.

They went out to the lift together and James pressed the button. Waiting for the lift to appear at their floor he said idly, 'How do you get on with Blair?'

Amanda examined the toes of her satin shoes. 'I find him a little—difficult to understand.'

James chuckled. 'Yes, in modern psychological jargon he's a complex personality. More so than his father was. His father, I'd say, was a simple man, a good man. The kind of old-fashioned employer who has his workers' interests at heart. Integrity, probity, moral principles—that was John Craddock. His son is a different type altogether. More'—he searched for the right word—'more flexible.'

The lift sucked them downwards silently. Amanda looked up at James with a puzzled little frown. 'But—but I don't understand; I thought you liked Blair. And trusted him. You *seem* to trust him.'

They reached the ground floor and James pulled back the lift door, smiling down at her. 'I'd trust Blair Craddock with everything I've got in the world,' he said simply.

It was a large party that met in the famous restaurant

some time later. The directors of the French company were all there and Amanda had to be introduced to their wives, who hadn't, of course, been at the morning's meeting. The senior director Monsieur Perrin had brought his daughter and her husband, and Pierre le Brun, the youngest of the firm, was accompanied by his son Raoul, a good-looking young man in his early twenties, with polished manners and a flattering gleam in his eyes when they rested on Amanda, which was most of the time. She found herself seated next to him at the long table in the glittering restaurant, with Monsieur Perrin on her other side.

If she hadn't known that Blair might be coming Amanda would have enjoyed herself. As it was, the dinner party seemed to go on around her as if she were present only as a kind of ghost. Everyone, she was aware, was being very nice to her, the women nodding and smiling across the table and leaning forward to make small remarks in English, which she felt they were using out of courtesy to her, not knowing that she spoke French almost as well as her father.

Monsieur Perrin, after one or two rather laboured compliments, turned his attention to James, sitting further down the table, and began to talk business, in spite of his wife's protests. That left Amanda open to Raoul's flattering attentions, which she received absently. She was only vaguely aware of the glittering surroundings, the dresses and jewels and perfumes, the men's elegant dinner suits, the hum of conversation, the noiseless tread of the waiters as they came and went and hovered unobtrusively.

Courses followed each other, luscious and mouthwatering. She was being served, Amanda supposed, with what could be the most inspired cuisine in the world. It was stupid and thankless not to let herself enjoy it, just because at any moment Blair Craddock might—just *might*—appear at that wide doorway far across the room. She forced herself to turn towards the amiable young man beside her and give her attention to what he was saying.

He leaned close to fill her champagne glass before the waiter could reach it. 'I have heard that you are about to join your father's firm. Is that so indeed? It would be most splendid.'

She assured him that it was so indeed, and added that she was sure she was going to find the work most interesting.

'And *I* am sure——' he smiled gallantly at her '—that your father's customers will find it no less—interesting. It is a happy chance that I, too, will be part of the family business when my last year at the university is completed.'

'You are a student?' She couldn't hide her surprise. This soigné young man in elegant dinner dress wasn't her idea of a modern student in any European country.

His mouth pulled wryly. 'You are thinking I look too—civilised, eh? It is entirely in your honour, I assure you, mademoiselle. My father tells me, "Raoul, Monsieur Dawson's daughter is very young and very beautiful, you must take trouble with your appearance so that you do not offend her." And so I brush my hair and wash my face and put on my best suit, you see? And you would not recognise the—how do you say it?—the scruffy student of this afternoon.'

She glanced at him uncertainly, not sure if he were fooling or not. But his eyes were dancing, admiring her, inviting her to share the joke, and she began to laugh too.

'Ah, that is better,' murmured Raoul close to her ear. 'The lovely Amanda is perhaps a little too *sérieuse*. When you come again to Paris with your father perhaps I may be allowed to show you some of our interesting places? We should have fun together, yes?'

Amanda sipped her champagne. 'Thank you,' she said demurely. 'I should enjoy that very much.'

His face came nearer, brushed lightly against her hair. 'Ah, so should I,' he whispered softly.

It was at that moment that she saw Blair making his way towards them. Her mouth went dry and her heart started to thump. She stared, wide-eyed, as he approached. She had known that he might come, but now she admitted that she hadn't really believed it, or been prepared for the shattering effect his sudden appearance always had on her. He was wearing a dinner jacket with a crisp white shirt. For the first time she was conscious of the dark, Celtic look of the man, a primitive strength and savage pride that his ancestors might have directed against the invaders, fighting grimly back in the wildness of their Welsh mountains. She smothered a giggle. This was Paris in the twentieth century, the home of culture and civilised life. But the fleeting impression remained and was even strengthened as she saw the way the women stirred and glanced up at him under their eyelashes as he passed.

A chair was brought for him beside the wife of the senior director, Madame Perrin, and he slipped into it, greeting the other members of the party, whom he evidently knew well already, apologising for his lateness, smiling and being his most charming self. His dark glance passed over Amanda, sitting close beside Raoul, and moved away again, giving her no special acknowledgement. Not that she would have expected it, she assured herself. All the same, an odd feeling of disappointment lingered in her.

'Ah, so the important Monsieur Craddock has arrived,' remarked Raoul, beside her. 'But where, I ask myself, has he left his most beautiful wife Juliet, on this occasion of celebration?'

Amanda blinked into the suave face. 'His wife? You must be mistaken. He's not married.'

'No? Ah, then I am wrong. When Monsieur Craddock visited my father's house recently he brought with him this lady. I understood she was his wife. So—they are not married?'

'Not yet,' said Amanda shortly, echoing the very words that James had used to her.

Raoul's brows rose and he nodded with man-of-the-world cynicism. 'Ah yes, I see.' He slid her a knowing look. 'Well, life is short and we must make the most of it, must we not?'

In the warm restaurant she felt suddenly cold. Raoul's meaning couldn't have been plainer and she shouldn't have been surprised that Blair and Juliet were lovers. But why, she wondered, did they have to go about it in such a furtive way, making the most of their trips abroad together? Why were they not married already, or at least formally engaged?

The dinner went on and on. Inevitably, as it was a celebration of a contract between two companies, the conversation drifted into 'shop' talk—of advance orders, delivery dates, markets, development plans. Even the wives, who earlier had tried to keep things on a light social level, gave up the attempt and joined in. They seemed to know a great deal about the business.

Raoul's hand touched Amanda's with a light pressure. 'We are the beginners, you and I, the *apprentis*. Soon we will have to take part in all this dull business talk, but until that time let us amuse ourselves together.'

She glanced down the table at Blair, who seemed deeply interested in something that Monsieur Perrin was expounding, and then gave the young Frenchman a brilliant smile. 'That would be fun,' she said, and sat back to enjoy the *café filtre*, and the *crème de menthe frappé*, which Raoul insisted on ordering for her.

Raoul was enjoying himself, she could see, trying out his new role as the young cosmopolitan executive. She could just see him in a few years' time, very like Pierre, his father, who was a real charmer. Amanda listened while Raoul talked amusingly of his friends and professors at the Sorbonne. 'We have to be political, you know,' he told her seriously, 'but there are things much more important than politics.' And he smiled into her eyes, telling her in no uncertain way that she was one of those things.

'Next year,' he told her, 'I shall be travelling with my father, and we shall give ourselves the pleasure of visiting *your* establishment, then I can see how my fellow *apprentie* is progressing, and we can renew our friendship, *oui?*'

'*Mais oui*, I shall look forward to it,' she said, giving the young man her most charming smile, which had the effect of rendering him speechless for a few moments. She was, she knew, flirting outrageously with him, and she also had to admit that it was for Blair's benefit. In some way that she couldn't explain, she had to try to annoy him, even to get her own back on him—although what he had done to merit her anger she wasn't at all clear about.

There was a movement at the end of the table and then Amanda saw that the celebration dinner was over. As they left the restaurant and went out on to the Rond Point, with its trees and fountains and swirl of cars in the brilliance of the lights, Raoul took Amanda's arm in his. 'The old ones will be going home,' he said, low at her ear. 'But how would you like to come on with me to a night club I know?'

Suddenly Blair was standing beside them. 'Your father is a little tired, Amanda,' he said brusquely. 'If you're quite ready we'll go back to the hotel.'

Raoul spoke up promptly, not releasing Amanda's arm. 'I have just suggested to Mademoiselle Amanda that we should go on to a night club, if she is agreeable.'

For a moment the two men eyed each other. In a way they were a little alike, both tall, both dark, both well-made and essentially masculine. But there the resemblance ended, Amanda thought. Raoul was merely practising being mature and worldly; Blair was formidably the real thing.

'I'm sure she would be charmed,' he said pleasantly, 'but we have to be up early in the morning to catch our flight, I'm sure you will understand that her father would prefer her to come back to the hotel with us.'

Raoul looked a little dashed, but he rose to the occasion

bravely. 'Of course.' He made a little formal bow over Amanda's hand and raised it to his lips. '*Au revoir*, mademoiselle, it has been enchanting.' The formality ceased as he grinned wickedly into her eyes. '*A bientôt!*'

The party was breaking up, going their separate ways. James was beside Amanda, a hand on her shoulder. 'Hullo, sweetheart, enjoyed yourself?' He looked towards Blair. 'Pierre has a spare seat in his car; he's offered to drop me at the hotel on his way home. Will you see Amanda back?'

'Delighted!' said Blair. He hooked his arm through Amanda's and a moment or two later she found herself being led firmly along the wide pavement of the Champs-Elysées beneath the broad-leaved plane trees which threw flickering shadows at their feet as the breeze rustled the leaves. 'Shall I try and find a taxi, or would you like to walk?' he asked. 'It's not very far.'

Amanda was fighting a small battle inside herself. On the one hand she was annoyed with Blair for being so high-handed about the way he had detached her from Raoul. Just as if she were a small girl being taken home from a party by a bored and unwilling elder brother! He really had been most rude, and Raoul had behaved beautifully, she told herself.

On the other hand, Blair's closeness, as they strolled along, was beginning to distil its potent magic into her bloodstream, arousing all the clamour in her limbs to move closer to him, to press herself against his hard body.

All around them streams of pedestrians interwove, walking in a leisurely fashion in the warm evening air, under the trees. As a knot of what were obviously tourists approached Amanda took the opportunity of drawing away from Blair, but as soon as the group had passed between them, chattering in a language Amanda did not recognise, he came close again.

'Too many bodies around here tonight,' he remarked. 'We'll cut across the gardens and round by the river; it isn't much further and it may even save a bit of time.'

He couldn't get her back to the hotel fast enough, could he? 'Oh yes, by all means let's hurry,' she said, and quickened her pace as they turned into a wide avenue with an expanse of gardens on either side.

Blair did not appear to lengthen his stride as he walked beside her, and he ignored her peevish remark completely. 'This is called the Avenue Winston Churchill,' he remarked placidly. 'They re-christened it after the war. Does that make you feel more at home?'

She drew a little further away from him. 'Why should I want to feel more at home? I'm enjoying myself in Paris.'

'Good! Splendid!' he said dryly. 'And looking so very soignée too!' He touched the soft lace of her blouse and his fingers moved lightly down to twitch a fold of the blue silk that foamed and dipped below her hips. Then he caught her waist and twirled her round to face him before she realised what he was going to do. For a split second she thought he was going to draw her closer into his arms and her knees felt weak and trembly. But he only leaned towards her and examined her hair and her face with minute care. At last he said, 'Yes—very nice! An improvement—if one were possible, which I doubt. Paris has done you proud.'

She felt a little like a rag doll he had picked up and tossed away. 'I'm glad you approve,' she said coldly. With a quick movement she wriggled away from the arm that still held her and marched on ahead of him.

In two strides he had caught her up. 'This way,' he said, 'it cuts off a corner.' This time he didn't take her by the arm, but clasped her hand and guided her into a side path.

There were fewer people here, mostly couples strolling along with their arms entwined, while further from the path dark shadowy forms on the grass suggested more intimate happenings. In the warm evening air, with the noise of traffic dulled to a murmur and the scents rising from the flower-beds, the whole atmosphere of the place was languorous and seductive, and Amanda wondered with a sinking feeling in the pit of her stomach just why Blair had suggested coming this way, and what she should do if he—if he——

'See that place over there?' His voice broke into her imaginings, calm and conversational. 'It's the Musée des Beaux Arts. Well worth a visit, I must take you there some time. It's called the Petit Palais. Its big brother, the Grand Palais, is over on the other side. I went to the motor show there once.'

Amanda peered through the trees towards the massive building, its many windows glinting in the lights from the avenue. 'How interesting,' she said woodenly.

'Isn't it?' His voice was softly mocking. He must have guessed all about the thoughts that had been going through her head, she thought in humiliation, and felt her cheeks begin to burn. 'Anything else of interest you would care to know about?' he went on in the tone of a travel-guide. 'We shall soon be reaching the Cours-la-Reine, so named because it was ordered by Marie de Valois, wife of Henri the Fourth in—er—the seventeenth century, I believe. From there you will have a view across the river towards the Quai d'Orsay and also have glimpses of the Eiffel Tower.' He chuckled. 'How am I doing?'

'It's all quite fascinating,' said Amanda distantly.

He was still holding her hand as they walked along and now he gave it an encouraging squeeze. 'Cheer up, poppet,' he urged. 'I know it would have been exciting to go off to a night club with your new friend Raoul—or rather, you *think* it would—but James really did want you back at the hotel with him. And we do have to consider him, don't we?'

So *that* was what he thought—that she was disappointed at having to leave Raoul and was sulking childishly at being deprived of a treat! She drew in a breath of relief. Much better that he should think that, rather than guess how desperately she was trying to fight off this abysmal longing to be in his arms, in the darkness, under the trees.

'Yes,' she said quickly. 'You're right, of course. This is James's day, we must do as he wants. Let's get back as soon as we can, shall we?'

For a moment he seemed to hesitate. Then he lowered his head and dropped a kiss on her hair. 'That's my girl,' he murmured. He took her arm again and they stepped out briskly towards the lights that marked the Place de la Concorde.

Afterwards, when she thought about it, Amanda remembered the flight next day as a nightmare blur, but at the beginning she sat beside James in the first-class compartment, looking down at the rather nondescript French landscape as it gave way to puffy white clouds, and decided that the trip had been a success. It had introduced her to some of the men with whom James would be working closely in the future. Particularly Raoul, she thought with a small smile. Raoul was rather a sweetie.

Below, the smooth oily greyness of the Channel came into sight through the clouds. She tried to pass the rest of the time by making up a future when somehow she had got over her crazy passion for Blair; when Blair had married Juliet; when she, Amanda, was having a wonderful time in Paris with Raoul. But she couldn't keep up the illusion. She kept coming back to her present surroundings and seeing the back of Blair's dark head as he sat across the aisle and a little in front of them. Once or twice, during the flight, he had turned and grinned at her as if reassuring her about something. Did he imagine she was scared of air travel? A timid little country girl. Pooh to that, she thought with fine disdain. Just wait until she had found her feet with the firm; she would be flying all over the world soon, she told herself extravagantly, promoting Caradawc wares.

How soon, she wondered, following that line of thought,

could she go to visit the mills and offices and see for herself what went on there and how the whole company functioned? She turned to her father. 'I was wondering when——' she began.

And then her heart seemed to stop beating.

James had slumped in his seat and was struggling for breath, making horrible little rasping noises. His face was ashen and there were drops of sweat on his forehead. His eyes were wide open and she saw the terror in them.

Impulsively she covered his hands with hers and found them cold and rigid. Some vague recollection of first-aid lessons at school came to her—something about reassurance. 'You're all right, darling,' she whispered urgently. 'You're all right. Just keep quite still.'

She managed to wriggle past him, reached forward and touched Blair's shoulder. As his head jerked round she said clearly, 'James—he's ill.'

Blair was on his feet immediately, and that was when everything began to become unreal. Later she remembered a stewardess hurrying forward, then going away and coming back with a steward. They were pushing up the armrests of the seat, lowering James back to a semi-reclining position. She heard a call go out over the loudspeakers for a doctor; saw a small bald man coming through from the rear compartment. Then the doctor and the steward were bending over James.

Blair pushed her into the seat he had vacated. 'Stay there, Amanda,' he said quietly. 'Everything's being done. They're giving him oxygen.' He rested a hand for a moment on her shoulder, then disappeared through a partition in the front of the cabin.

Amanda was only vaguely aware of the stir among the other passengers. A middle-aged woman in the next seat said sympathetically, 'Your father, is it, my dear? Try not to worry too much—my husband had his attack a year ago and he's as good as new now. They always look awful at first—I know I was terrified when Frederick collapsed. Here, have a sip of my brandy.' She held the glass to Amanda's lips.

Blair came back. 'They're radioing for an ambulance to meet the plane,' he said. 'You go with James in the ambulance, will you, Amanda? My car's parked at Heathrow, so I'll find which hospital they're taking him to and follow on. We'll be in quite soon now.'

Blair took charge of everything. Sitting in the ambulance, holding James's hand in hers, some half an hour later, Amanda wondered how on earth she would have coped without Blair. It just didn't bear thinking about.

She told him so a little later, in the hospital. They were sitting together in an alcove off one of the main corridors. Nurses passed by, in ones and twos, young doctors in long white coats, porters pushing trolleys, all the ceaseless traffic of a large hospital. It reminded Amanda of when Gran had been taken ill and rushed to hospital. She had sat waiting then, just as she was sitting now, with the same sick feeling in her stomach. But then she had been alone. Now she had Blair sitting beside her.

She said impulsively, 'I can't help thinking how lucky it was that you were there when it happened. I know it's cowardly of me, but I don't know how I could have coped if I'd been on my own.'

He was leaning forward, his hands clasped between his knees, looking down at the floor. 'It wasn't luck,' he said.

She stared at the bent, dark head. 'What do you mean?'

He turned his head to look up at her. 'It was arranged. James phoned me after the meeting yesterday and asked me to drop everything and come to Paris.'

'Yes, I know, he told me. He thought it would be a good idea for you to join in the celebrations.'

'No, it wasn't quite like that.' He straightened himself on the leather bench seat, folding his arms. 'You'd better know the truth, Amanda. He'd been having symptoms. He had a feeling that this——' he looked down the corridor to where they had hurried the trolley with James upon it almost an hour ago '—might happen.'

She was appalled. 'You mean he *knew*—and he never said anything to me? He still carried on—the long meeting in the morning—that dinner last night?'

Blair nodded soberly. 'That's how he's made. James doesn't give up. But this time he was scared; scared not for himself but for you. Scared that if he were taken ill on the trip you might have to cope on your own. He said, Drop everything and get over here as soon as you can. So that you can look after her if the worst happens.'

She was silent for a long time, biting her lip, and there were tears in her eyes. She said shakily, 'I didn't ask—I didn't expect—that kind of love and consideration from him.'

He looked down at her thoughtfully, his arms still folded, and the expression on his face was unreadable. At last he said rather dryly, 'You don't have any choice in these matters, you know.'

'Oh!' she gasped. She studied his face, so calm, so controlled. 'What a horrid thing to say! Do you think I'd—I'd reject what he offers me? I'm grateful for his love, can't you understand that? I'd do anything—anything for him —to help him get better.'

A faint smile pulled at his mouth, a smile that seemed to her sceptical. 'Would you?' he said quietly. 'Would you really? Well, maybe I'll hold you to that, my child.'

Before she could ask him what he meant a young black nurse came up and looked from one to the other. 'Mr Craddock?'

Blair stood up immediately. 'Yes?'

'Will you come with me, please?'

Amanda was on her feet too. 'My—my father?' she stammered. 'Is he——?'

'Your father is conscious and Doctor is with him. Will

you wait, please? And Mr Craddock, will you come with me.' She was kind but firm.

Blair turned to Amanda with a slight shrug. 'I'll be back,' he said, and followed the nurse down the corridor.

Amanda couldn't sit still. She paced up and down the alcove—three steps one way, three steps back—over and over again, watching the clock on the opposite wall of the corridor, the minute hand turning in tiny jerks—five minutes—ten——

At last Blair was coming back and she ran to meet him. 'Well, what do you think? What do the doctors think?'

He put an arm round her and led her along the corridor, the way they had come in. 'They've done an electrocardiogram, that's the first thing, and they don't seem too unhappy, but it's too early to say anything. They say the next thing is blood studies and that's going to take two or three hours. They told me we might as well go away and have something to eat and come back again.'

She stopped, pulling back against his arm. 'But can't I see him? Why could you see him and not me?'

He said gently, 'He asked for me, Amanda, there was something on his mind.'

'Business?' she said. Would he still be worrying about business even if he was—was——?

Blair urged her on. 'No, not business, and you can see him later on, when we come back. They said so. Now look, there's a coffee bar along the road—come on.'

'But——' She still hung back.

'Come on, kitten,' he urged again. 'You'll feel better when you've had some food. And besides,' he added with an odd glance at her under his dark lashes, 'I've got something to say to you. Something rather important.'

CHAPTER SEVEN

AT the café the lunch-time rush was over, but the dingy room was still three-quarters full and a smell of frying hung on the air. 'Look, there's an empty table by the window,' said Blair. 'You go and nab that and I'll bring coffee and sandwiches.' He wrinkled his nose at the tired-looking plates of sandwiches behind their glass partitions. 'Ham or cheese?' he asked. 'I should think they'd both taste approximately the same.'

Amanda blinked at him. How could he look so ordinary, just as if this frightening thing hadn't happened? 'Oh— anything,' she said, and made for the table by the window.

'Blair——' she began, when he had set the plates and cups on the table and slid into the seat opposite. 'What——'

He pointed to the sandwiches before her. 'Eat first, questions afterwards.'

She shrugged and bit into a cheese sandwich. Surprisingly, she found she was hungry and she finished both the sandwiches, helped down by coffee. 'Now,' she said, 'tell me. It was a heart attack, wasn't it?'

Blair nodded soberly. 'Oh yes, and he was lucky.'

'*Lucky?*'

'Yes, lucky. He's survived the first critical time and that's the most important thing. The doctors won't commit themselves at this stage, of course, but I've learned a bit about these things; two chaps I've known have had coronaries recently and made good recoveries.'

The weight that seemed to have settled permanently in her chest lightened a little. She hadn't realised quite how tense she had been, or how much James had come to mean to her in such a short time.

'And what will happen now? How long will they keep him in hospital?'

'Ssh! Not so fast!' He smiled at her. 'But all being well it'll probably only be a matter of days—a week or so perhaps—before they let him out. After that I imagine it'll be quite a long convalescence. Rest. No smoking. No stress. That's the usual drill.'

She leaned across the table, clasping her hands eagerly. 'I can look after him when he gets home. I'd like to do that.'

Blair looked at her briefly, then he sipped his coffee in thoughful silence, as if he were trying to slow her down, to warn her against a too-easy optimism. At last he said, 'It's the No Stress part that bothers me.'

She nodded, biting her lip. 'Yes, I see what you mean. It's not so easy with James, is it?'

'Indeed it isn't.' His eyes were fixed on hers with that narrowed, deep blue glint behind their thick lashes. She felt suddenly breathless; even now, when her thoughts were with her father, this man had a disturbing power over her emotions.

'He's worrying, Amanda,' he said. 'That's why he asked to see me.'

'Oh dear! About the French deal? Has he forgotten that it's all settled?'

He shook his head. '*Not* about the French deal.' He paused deliberately. 'About you.'

'Me? Oh, surely——' She made a dismissive gesture. 'Why should he worry about me? I'm here, aren't I, and I promised him I'd stay.'

Blair's mouth pulled down expressively at the corners. 'Use your imagination, kitten. What do you think is the primary worry for a man of his age who has sole responsibility for a young daughter who's very lovely and desirable, and whom he adores?'

She felt the blood hot in her cheeks. 'Oh, but that's absurd! Surely he doesn't think I'd—I'd go off the rails in some way.' Garbled pictures of delinquent daughters hovered unpleasantly in her mind. 'I'm just not that sort of person.'

'No,' said Blair dryly, 'I don't think that's what's bothering him.'

'Then what is?'

'Just this—that once you're out in the world on your own, so to speak, you'll be the focus of attraction for every man in sight, eligible and ineligible; desirable and undesirable. He's afraid that you're much too young and inexperienced to be put at risk like that. He knows already what a tender heart you have and that you're quite likely to be swayed by the wrong type of man.'

'Did he say all that?'

A faint smile touched Blair's long, mobile mouth. 'Hardly. It needed only a word or two—I got the message.'

Amanda said rather bitterly, 'You would, wouldn't you? It squares with your own opinion of me.'

'We-ell——' He pretended to consider that. 'I'd say you got off to a slightly shaky start, but I have hopes for you. As you once told me, you learn fast.'

She remembered exactly when she said that to him, on that first night in his apartment, and she avoided his eyes. Was that the shaky start he was referring to? Was he thinking of her naïve, trusting response to his lovemaking? Or the episode with Christopher French? Or the flirtation with Raoul yesterday that she had certainly encouraged?

She frowned and pushed together the crumbs on her plate. 'Do you really believe that this worry about me—if it's as serious as you seem to think—could affect his chances of recovery?'

'I think it well might. He wouldn't have sent for me otherwise. I think it's been on his mind ever since you came and he saw for himself—well, let's say that he got to know you. As I said, he seems to have survived the first few critical hours, but there's a long road ahead after that and ...' he shrugged.

'But what can I do?' Amanda said rather desperately. 'I can't very well lock myself up, can I?'

He shook his head at her, smiling his calm smile. 'I don't think that will be necessary. I think I've done the trick —set his mind at rest, I mean.' He paused, looking straight into her eyes. 'I've just told James that I've asked you to marry me.'

She stared at him. The café, with its shabby furniture, the glass cases and coffee urns, the customers chattering or reading their newspapers, everything had gone out of focus. Only Blair's face, dark and relentlessly confident, was real to her, and on it she could find no clue to his feelings.

'Did you say—*marry* me?'

'That's right,' he said. 'It seemed a good idea. In fact, it was the only thing I could think of. I was fairly sure that James would be happy about it—that he'd trust you to me.'

The first shock was wearing off now. More to gain time than anything else she said, 'It won't do him very much good when you have to tell him that I've declined your offer.'

'I've taken care of that,' he said. 'Another cup of coffee?'

'No, thank you. What do you mean, taken care of it?' Her voice rose.

But he had carried his cup away to the counter and she had to wait for her answer until he came back. When he had settled himself opposite again she repeated the question.

He sat for a moment or two, cradling his cup in long, slender fingers, looking down into it. Then he raised his head and said slowly, giving his words weight, 'I *had* to reassure James somehow. I saw the fear in his eyes and I knew he thought he was going to die. He had sent for me to ask me to look after you. It wasn't enough, I reckoned, just to say Yes, I would. So I told him I'd asked you to marry me and that you'd said Yes.'

She drew in a sharp breath, but he went on calmly, 'It was quite dramatic. As soon as I said it he smiled and his whole body relaxed. I wish you could have seen it.'

Amanda was staring at him rather wildly. 'But he couldn't have believed you. He knows you're going to marry Juliet—he told me so. Well, as good as told me.'

'Yes, I know. But I think I was able to set his mind at rest on that point too.'

'You mean—you're not engaged to Juliet?'

'How can I be,' said Blair patiently, 'when I'm engaged to you?'

'But what will she think—how will she feel——?' She was remembering Blair and Juliet together that day they had all lunched in London, before Juliet left for New York; the looks of understanding and closeness that had passed between them. 'You can't possibly——'

His mouth hardened and she felt a qualm of fear. Nobody told Blair Craddock what he could, or could not, do. 'I told you,' he said tersely. 'There's no problem about Juliet.' And she could take that how she liked.

He was watching her closely. 'Well,' he said at last, 'will you back me up? We both want James to get better, don't we?'

She nodded, pressing her lips together tightly.

'So?'

'So I suppose I've no choice, have I?'

'Good!' He finished his coffee without haste. He looked like a man who has got his own way and is feeling very pleased with himself. 'Shall we get back to the hospital, then, if you're ready?'

They walked down the wide, busy street in silence, while traffic and pedestrians streamed past. Amanda glanced up at Blair, very tall and dark and looking unapproachable. Perhaps he was thinking of Juliet and how he was going to explain to her. Impulsively she put a hand on his arm and said, 'Making sure that James has the best chance of getting better is the really important thing, isn't it? Everything else can be sorted out later on.'

The grimness went out of his face. 'For one so young,' he said, 'you have great good sense, kitten.' And in the middle of the busy London pavement he bent down and kissed her.

Her heart shook, and out of habit she threw a startled glance around, for if it had happened in King's Holton the word would be all round the village within minutes that Amanda Dawson was being kissed by a man right out there in the street. But in London, of course, nobody took the slightest notice except Amanda herself, who for no very good reason felt that things had taken a sudden turn for the better.

The report at the hospital was encouraging. 'He's got through the first critical period without a setback,' the doctor told them. 'He was very tense when he came in, but fortunately he seems more relaxed now.'

Amanda glanced at Blair and he nodded as if to say, 'It worked!'

'May I see him?' she asked the doctor.

'Surely, but only for a minute, mind.' He called a passing nurse. 'Nurse, will you take Miss Dawson to the coronary unit to see her father, please. One minute only.' He glanced towards Blair and then added to Amanda, 'Your fiancé had better wait, this time.'

Amanda followed the young nurse in her blue and white crispness down the long corridor. Your fiancé—how strange it sounded! Somehow warm and reassuring though, even if it were hardly accurate.

When she saw James, lying so still and greyish-white in his bed, surrounded by the alarming life-saving apparatus of modern medicine, she needed all the reassurance she could get. He looked so much worse than she had expected. She went forward and dropped on her knees beside the bed, covering his hands with her own, unable to speak for a moment.

He turned his eyes towards her without moving his head and she thought she saw in them a ghost of his old quizzical, monkey-eyed smile. She leaned over and kissed him. 'Hullo, darling, how are you? You're looking ever so much better than I expected,' she lied bravely. 'We'll soon have you home again and I'll be able to look after you.'

His eyes rested on her face as if he were taking in every tiny detail of it. 'You—and Blair,' he whispered carefully. 'It's—wonderful. You're happy, Mandy?'

The little pet-name made her choke suddenly. 'Blissful,' she said, hoping that the tears in her eyes would look like tears of happiness. 'But you must hurry up and get yourself better and then we'll all have such good times together.'

The nurse hovered and Amanda stood up and kissed James again. 'I'll come back soon, darling,' she said. At the door she turned and smiled and saw him try to smile back.

Blair was waiting outside and she had to stand still for a moment until she could force back the tears. He put a comforting arm round her and they walked back along the corridor. 'He looks awful,' said Amanda. 'Do you really think he'll get better?'

'I'm sure he will,' Blair said steadily. 'He's got everything on his side. He's only forty-nine, has no money worries, and has just acquired a beautiful daughter. To say nothing of an eligible son-in-law-to-be!' He touched her cheek lightly. 'Come on, Amanda, let's see that smile.'

She gave him a rather watery grin. 'What do we do now? I'd like to stay here, to be near him. Would they let me?'

He said doubtfully, 'I expect so, but I've been having a word with Sister and she agrees with me that it would be much better to be somewhere you can rest. James's flat is only a short taxi-ride away. I've got keys to it—he allows me to use it when I'm in town—and I've left the phone number with Sister, who's promised to get in touch with you immediately if anything—unexpected should happen.'

He had his hand on her elbow and she found herself being

led towards the entrance door. 'So I think that's the best place for you to be just at present.'

She stopped abruptly and he stopped beside her. 'I'd rather stay here,' she said.

He said patiently, 'Yes, I know, kitten, but I think this way is best.' His voice had its masterful note. She could argue if she had the courage, but she had a feeling that if she did she would be sure to lose in the end.

'All right,' she said wearily. 'Let's go.'

While they drove the short distance to the flat Amanda tried to concentrate on the streets she could make out between the traffic. She was aware of a compulsive need to show Blair that she wasn't a child and could look after herself, so the sooner she was able to find her own way round London the better.

But in the end she gave up trying to remember landmarks. Blair drove expertly, swooping in and out of the moving maze of cars, through junctions and round corners, until her head was in a whirl and she closed her eyes, only to open them again when the car finally stopped outside the row of tall houses in the comparative quiet of a small square.

'We'll go up, then.' Blair lifted Amanda's travelling case from the back seat. He must have remembered to bring it from Heathrow, she supposed. She herself had forgotten all about it until this moment. No wonder he treated her like an infant, she thought dismally.

The outside of the house was a period piece, with its Georgian windows and wrought-iron railings to area and balcony. But inside it had been expertly converted to the modern standards of luxury living, with thick carpets everywhere, walls panelled in light wood, and white doors with discreet bronze name-plates on them.

Amanda looked round with interest as they came out of the lift on the third floor. She hadn't taken particular notice of anything when she was here before, but now she was going to make it her home while she was in London and the prospect held out an exciting challenge.

Blair led the way down a silent corridor and opened one of the white doors. He put her case down on a chair in the sitting room. 'You'll be all right here, kitten, you'll be able to manage on your own?' he asked doubtfully.

Her excitement suddenly exploded in anger. 'Oh, don't *fuss*, Blair! Really! Anyone would think I was eight, not eighteen.'

She glared at him and saw the dark eyebrows go up and a gleam come into his eyes. She held his look until she couldn't hold it any longer; then she turned to the window and stood staring down at the grass of the square far below while it blurred before her eyes.

He came up behind her and put both hands on her shoulders. 'I don't for one moment think you're eight, Amanda. Quite definitely not.'

His hands slid deliberately down her arms and closed round her breasts beneath the open jacket of her white suit. She stood quite still, unable to move or speak, her heart pounding so hard against her ribs that she was sure he would be able to hear it. He could certainly feel it under his hands, she thought confusedly, and know the turmoil he was setting up inside her. She waited for him to turn her round to face him, to take her in his arms, and every nerve and cell in her body ached for him to do just that.

He moved away from her and said briskly, 'Now, to make plans.' He glanced at his watch. 'Extraordinary as it may seem it's only just after four o'clock. You'd better stay here by the phone and I'll go out to Fortnums and stock up on provisions. We can have a meal of sorts here and then I'll have to leave you on your own and get back. O.K.?'

'O.K.' Somehow she managed to speak lightly, to turn and smile at him just as if that intimate caress meant nothing more to her than it had evidently done to him. He had meant it kindly, no doubt, as an encouragement to her pathetic lack of poise. As her eyes followed him to the door she wished unhappily that the events of the last few days had never happened at all and that she was safely back in the cottage at King's Holton, planning an unambitious career for herself as a shorthand-typist.

Blair was back within an hour. He dumped two bulging carriers on the table and pulled it up in front of the window. 'There,' he said with satisfaction, 'we can watch the sun go down while we eat, and pretend we're back in Paris.'

He went into the tiny kitchen and came back with plates and cutlery, glasses and a corkscrew, while Amanda unpacked the bags and arranged the contents on the table— a tub of fresh salmon in a bed of crisp lettuce leaves; various smaller tubs of exotic salads in creamy dressings; fresh peaches; raspberries; cream; a selection of cheeses; a long baton of French bread; a pale slab of butter surrounded by crushed ice.

'It's a banquet,' she said as Blair drew the cork from a bottle of wine and filled their glasses.

He took a sip consideringly. 'Not at the right temperature, I'm afraid, but apart from that, quite good. Here's to James's rapid recovery,' he said, and they drank the toast together.

'And before we go any further, let me give you this.' He groped in his inside pocket and drew out a small leather box. 'Chosen in a hurry,' he said in an offhand voice, 'but I hope you won't dislike it too much. If you do, we can change it.' He flicked open the lid to disclose a glittering diamond cluster ring. 'Will it do?' he asked quite anxiously. 'I had to get the woman in Garrards to advise me. I don't exactly make a habit of buying engagement rings. Put it on and let's see.' He took her hand and pushed the ring on to her third finger. 'A perfect fit—couldn't be better. What do you think of it, Amanda?'

She looked at the beautiful thing on her finger and the

words flashed into her mind: 'A diamond is forever.' She thrust the thought away, because of course the words could hardly apply less, and said rather woodenly, 'I like it very much. I'll take great care of it.'

He was looking hard at her with an odd expression on his face. Then he lifted his glass again. 'Here's to you, Amanda, and thank you for your co-operation in our little scheme. Without it, I truly believe we might not be celebrating James's recovery tonight.'

Co-operation—what a dry, formal word to choose! Well, she could be formal too. She said, 'I'm very glad it seems to have worked. It would have been bitterly disappointing if our plans had been spoilt, my father's and mine.'

'Plans?' he echoed, mildly interested, as they sat down opposite each other at the table by the window.

'Oh yes,' she said airily, 'we'd got it all worked out on the flight to Paris, and James took me with him yesterday morning to the meeting. I'm going to be taken into the firm and learn all about it—my father's side of it, that is, not yours—and eventually be able to help him. He has his own secretary, of course, but I should have a different job—sort of personal assistant.' She chattered on as they ate, enlarging on her training, inventing ambitions much loftier than had ever occurred to her.

She noticed that Blair had become completely silent. 'Of course, he would have consulted you, I'm sure, before anything definite was arranged,' she ended up. 'Would you have any objection to my joining the firm?'

He raised his eyebrows. 'Me? No, why should I? He'll need all the help he can get when he gets back into harness again.' He looked at her closely. 'Do you see yourself as a career woman, then?'

'Oh yes, most definitely.' She met his eyes with her clear, grey-blue gaze, thinking that she was carrying this off rather well. 'It's exactly what I've always wanted—only I must admit I expected to be starting as a lowly shorthand-typist and now here I am coming in near the top as the boss's daughter. Most immoral!' She spoke on a laugh.

Blair broke a hunk of crisp French bread and looked at it. 'You hadn't considered marriage as a career, then?'

'Oh, I don't think I'd considered marriage as a *career*. Girl's don't, these days, do they? Marriage is something that you do if you fall in love and it's impossible *not* to get married and be together all the time. Not something planned and organised, like a career. At least, that's how I see it.'

There was a short silence. Then he reached across the table and took her hand, with his diamonds on the slim third finger. 'Well, you'll have to let me know if you happen to fall in love in the near future. This——' he touched the ring '—might prove slightly off-putting to the lucky man.'

'Oh, I don't suppose it'll happen for ages. There are so many interesting things to do first, before I even think of settling down. But before anything else I mean to see that James gets really better. He doesn't seem to have much idea of looking after himself, so I'll have to do it for him. Or——' she paused doubtfully, as the idea suddenly occurred to her '—do you suppose Mrs French will want to take over when he gets back home?'

'Elaine?' Blair's mouth turned down. 'I'd think it highly unlikely. I can't see that lady giving support and succour to an invalid. In fact, I saw her when I had James's S.O.S. from Paris and I could see she was quite horrified at the idea that he might be going to be ill. She was talking rather vaguely about plans to take over a boutique here in London, owned by some friend of hers, so I shouldn't be surprised if she's on her way out.'

'Oh, good!' Amanda breathed a sigh of relief. 'That would be super. She—I—well, we didn't get on very well. She didn't like me.'

'She wouldn't,' said Blair dryly. 'You spoilt all her plans.'

'To marry James, you mean? She hinted to me that she was going to.'

Blair laughed aloud. 'She was trying to scare you off. I

realised that after her little ploy at the party. Dressing you up like that. A lamb to the slaughter, weren't you, kitten?' He seemed highly amused.

Every detail of that disastrous evening flashed into Amanda's mind. She could almost believe she was back in the dimly lit bedroom with this man's arms around her, pinning her down on to the bed. She could almost feel again the weight of his body on hers and at the memory the blood rose up to flood her cheeks. She bent her head over the peach she was peeling and said nothing.

He was watching her. 'I'm sorry, Amanda,' he said. 'I shouldn't have said that. I forgot you weren't like other girls.'

He paused for a moment, but she didn't look up. 'Now,' he said matter-of-factly, getting to his feet, 'I'll show you how the coffee percolator works. It's one of those new gadgets. Then I must be on my way.'

She followed him to the kitchen. Her knees were like elastic, but she must not on any account let him realise how she was feeling. Better that he should think she was youthfully embarrassed than that he should guess the hunger she felt to have his arms holding her.

She leaned against the kitchen door. 'Aren't you going to stay for coffee?' she said.

'I think not. I shan't get back to the office until nearly ten as it is.'

'You're not going back to work *tonight*?'

His smile was sardonic. 'My dear girl, there's no such thing as an eight-hour day when you're an executive, as you'll find out for yourself quite soon, now you've decided to be a career woman. Look, you put the coffee in here and the water here, set the timer and——'

She wasn't listening. She almost said she didn't want coffee if she had to drink it alone, but that would look as if she were pleading with him to stay.

He telephoned the hospital then, and had a reassuring

report on James's condition. Relaying the message to Amanda he added, 'Things are getting under control now. I've left you a key of the flat on the desk over there. How are you fixed for money?'

She looked into the purse in her white shoulder bag. 'Twenty francs.' She pulled a face. 'And I left my post office book back at Radneys.'

'No problem.' He counted notes from a leather wallet. 'I'll leave you fifty pounds—that'll be enough to go on with. And I'll be back tomorrow afternoon, as soon as I can get away, to see how you are getting on.' He looked at her with a small frown. 'I don't like the idea of leaving you alone in London, but I can't see any alternative.'

She said lightly, 'Oh goodness, I'll be perfectly all right. Surely *you* don't imagine I'm made of precious porcelain, even if James does?'

He made no reply to that, merely went on scribbling on the note-pad by the telephone, and she was left feeling that she had said something stupid and provocative which he chose to ignore.

Then he picked up his briefcase. 'I've left the phone number of Radneys there and of my office too, in case you should need to get in touch.'

'You think of everything, don't you?' she said snappily.

Blair grinned at her in a maddening way. 'I'm not going to fight with you, kitten. We're partners, remember? No, don't come down with me, I must rush away now. Au revoir, Amanda, I'm sure you'll manage splendidly.' He touched her shoulder, dropped a light kiss on her hair and was gone.

He didn't wait for the lift but ran down the stairs. She went back into the flat and stood at the window, looking down on the tops of the parked cars in the square below, not quite sure which of the glossy roofs belonged to Blair's car. A few moments later he appeared on the pavement and the sight of him down there, so remote and yet so utterly familiar—every detail of his tall figure—gave her a sharp twist inside that was almost a pain.

Her hand went to the window-frame, ready to wave when he looked up. But he didn't look up. He ran across the wide pavement, climbed into his car and slammed the door. Then he reversed out briskly and drove away.

Amanda watched the car until it had passed out of sight on the other side of the square. Then, hunching her shoulders as if she were cold, she went slowly back to the kitchen to switch off the coffee-maker.

That night Amanda was a long time going to sleep and she wakened in the unfamiliar bedroom to find the sun pouring in and her watch saying ten o'clock. Her first thought was for James, lying in his hospital bed with the teeming city streets between them, and she was filled with anxiety and guilt. She should have stayed with him at the hospital; she shouldn't have let Blair take charge of her and bring her here.

She padded into the sitting room. The white telephone on the desk had an ominous, waiting look. She dialled the hospital number that Blair had written on the pad and waited, her inside churning with nerves, her hands cold and damp.

A very far-away voice said something she couldn't make out, but she asked hopefully for the Coronary Unit and when another voice said clearly, 'Yes?' she gabbled, 'This is Amanda Dawson, I hope I'm not too early ringing up. My father——' Something caught her throat.

'Ah yes.' The voice came nearer, became kind and personal. 'Your father had a good night, Miss Dawson, and his condition is satisfactory.'

'Oh, thank you. Thank you so much.' Amanda fumbled the receiver back on to its cradle and drew in a deep breath as she went over to the window. It must have rained in the night, for the wet pavements below were silver in the sunlight and little wisps of steam were rising from them; the square of grass looked fresh and tenderly green. Two small children were playing with a red and white striped ball down there while a nanny sat on a seat with her knitting.

Amanda felt her spirits rising. In spite of everything that had happened it was exciting to be in London on her own—it was a challenge. She would, she vowed, manage so well and be so organised and efficient that Blair would have to take back all that 'kitten' stuff and admit that she was grown-up and quite capable of looking after herself.

Just for a moment she remembered Juliet, so competent and self-assured, jetting off alone to New York. Juliet, so warm and lovely and charming and friendly. She pushed the thought away. She wasn't competing with Juliet; she would lose that game before she began.

When she had showered and dressed and breakfasted off hunks of the French loaf (which was getting somewhat stale) and the remainder of the carton of milk (because she didn't dare cope with the coffee-maker until she'd had time to study it) she tidied up the flat, washed her cup and plate in the minuscule sink in the kitchen and sat down to make plans.

She would need to buy a few things if she were to be in London for several days—undies and pantyhose certainly, and a couple of light summer dresses that she could wear all day. She only had the white dress and jacket she had taken to Paris and the fabulous evening dress James had bought her there.

She would also need to stock in with food. Lunch was no problem; she could find a café somewhere, but she would have to have a meal ready for when Blair arrived. She looked dubiously through the kitchen doorway at the white microwave oven, which seemed to be the only cooking equipment, and wondered if she dared experiment with it. She would have to see if there were an instruction book anywhere about. The very last thing she wanted to do was to confront Blair with a badly-cooked meal, when she had decided to impress him with her efficiency. Better be on the safe side and get something cold, like they had had last night.

Having planned to her satisfaction, she checked on her white shoulder-bag: handkerchief, comb, key of the flat, purse containing the fifty pounds Blair had provided her with. Then she slipped on the short white jacket of her suit, and—making sure the door was securely locked—ran down the staircase and out into the sunlit square with a spring in her step and the light of adventure shining in her clear, grey-blue eyes.

The promise of the morning was kept for a time. She found her way to Oxford Street, where she bought a plan of London and discovered that the hospital was within reasonable walking distance. Once there, she finally managed to locate her father's whereabouts in the huge, bewildering building, and, after an encouraging word with the Sister-in-Charge, she was given permission to sit with him for a few minutes.

He looked a different man this morning. 'It seems they can patch me up after all, Mandy,' he said, and today his monkey-eyed smile had some of its old mischief. He paused to collect his breath. 'Best news I've heard—you and Blair —such a surprise—did me a world of good.'

'I'm glad,' she said, squeezing his hand, trying to look blissful as a newly-engaged girl should look. 'It was a get-well-soon present. That was why we announced it so suddenly.'

Because she didn't want to go on talking about Blair she told him of the plans for her to stay at the flat, enthusing about it and how she was going to enjoy playing house there. Then she outlined her programme for this afternoon's shopping. 'I've got my map,' she patted her shoulder-bag. 'I'll find somewhere for lunch.'

'Try the National Gallery,' said James. 'Easy to find and they have good sandwiches.'

So when she had kissed him goodbye and promised to return later on, and perhaps bring Blair with her, she consulted her map and made for Trafalgar Square. She found it without difficulty and it was almost solid with people—and pigeons. There seemed to be about an equal number of each. The sun was blazing down, turning the fountains into sprays of flashing brilliance. The holiday spirit was everywhere. Cameras clicked as tourists posed in front of the stone lions, or gingerly balanced pigeons on their shoulders. Men were in their shirts, or stripped to the waist; children wore even less. The women were gay in their flowered summer dresses. Everyone looked hot but happy and Amanda's spirits chimed in with the general atmosphere of a mass of people being let off the hook and determined to have a good time. This was London. It was hot and noisy and crowded, but it was fun.

But she must certainly buy something cooler to wear, she decided, easing her way towards what her map had told her was the National Gallery, on the far side of the square. One dress at least, she thought, as she waited at the traffic lights to cross the street; she had quite enough money to buy that, as well as food and taxi fares. She would find out about the buses and tube trains later on.

The lights changed and she reached the steps of the Gallery and hitched her white shoulder-bag further up, comfortably aware of the fifty pounds in crisp notes that Blair had given her last night, reposing in her purse.

Then her blood ran cold. The bag was gaping open. Her purse, with all the money and the key to the flat, had gone. Nothing remained but a white plastic comb and an old Devon bus ticket.

At first she couldn't believe it and scrabbled in the bag frantically as if the long wallet-purse had somehow managed to hide itself there, but of course it hadn't. She sat down on the steps of the Gallery, feeling sick. There was something particularly horrible about the thought that while she had been crossing the square among the happy, noisy crowd, a hand had slipped the catch of her bag—groped inside——

She sat staring numbly in front of her. Even London itself seemed to have changed. The heat was oppressive now; the square looked dusty and grimy and one of the fountains had stopped working. The litter of the crowds was everywhere, flowing out of rubbish bins, piling up in corners: cigarette packets; chocolate-bar wrappings, beer-can rings. And from somewhere close a young child began to scream with the shrill tone of over-tiredness.

Amanda got to her feet. A wildly successful career girl she would be, she thought bitterly, when she couldn't even look after her own purse in the middle of a London crowd! No hope of finding the thief among all that mass of humanity, but she supposed she had better report her loss, and then find her way back to the flat. She sighed deeply and began to look around for a policeman.

It was almost two hours later when the caretaker, using his own key, opened the door of James's flat and regarded Amanda's small, weary face with long-suffering disapproval.

'You didn't ought to be here on your own, miss,' he told her severely. He was an elderly man with thin grey hair, furrowed cheeks and a drawn-down mouth. 'I told Mr Craddock so when he brought you here yesterday. Why, she's nothing but a child, I said. And what are you going to do now, with Mr Dawson ill in 'orspital and you losing all your money and everything?'

Amanda leaned against the door post, not replying, and the caretaker went on, 'Well, you'd better come down and arsk me if you want anything. Though I'm not promising nothing, mind, I've got enough to do as it is without——'

'Thank you,' Amanda said in a small tired voice. 'Now, if I may go inside, please?'

The clear, blue-grey gaze must have retained something

of its impact, for the man moved aside immediately. 'I can't let you keep my key, miss,' he said in a less aggressive tone. 'Regulations.'

'It doesn't matter,' said Amanda. 'Thank you for letting me in.' She went inside and closed the door.

The flat felt airless. She threw the windows wide and drew herself a long drink of water; then she peeled off her clothes and stood under the shower in the bathroom, letting the tepid drops sluice over her head and tired, hot body. After that she rubbed her hair partly dry, slipped into the filmy pale blue robe she had taken to Paris, and sat in the sitting room, trying to work out what to do.

It wasn't easy. The worst thing was that she had promised James to visit him again today and she didn't see how she was going to get to the hospital. She had no money for a taxi, or even a bus or tube—always supposing she could find the right one. To walk would take more than an hour from here, she calculated, and her feet were aching so badly that she doubted if she would get there, even if she started out.

Then there was the matter of food. There was nothing left to eat in the flat except the remainder of last night's meal. Enough, she supposed, to keep her alive until she could get some money from somewhere. If Blair didn't come back today she was sunk, and if he did come back, having to confess to him that she had got herself into such a muddle seemed the final straw.

Normally, Amanda wasn't a weepy girl, but suddenly the whole wretched situation was too much for her. Dropping her head in her hands, she wept.

The sound of the outside door of the flat opening made her sit up straight.

'Hullo, kitten,' said Blair's voice from behind her. And —as he came across the room—'You really should lock the outside door, you know. Anyone could walk in.'

She kept her head resolutely turned away from him,

biting her lip to force back the humiliating tears. The worst thing of all was for Blair to find her weakly snivelling, she thought, furious with herself.

He came and stood in front of her. 'Amanda, what's the matter? It's not James, is it? I phoned the hospital and they said he was getting on well.'

She fastened her gaze on the ends of his tie; it was deep vibrant blue, the colour of his eyes, its silk shining smoothly against the crisp white of his shirt. She shook her head dumbly.

'Then what?' He reached out and tipped up her chin. 'Come on, kitten, let's have it.'

Her eyes met his and slid away again. 'I've had all the money you gave me stolen out of my handbag.'

To add to her desolation he laughed aloud. 'Is *that* all? I was imagining frightful things when I saw you.'

Her mouth shook. 'It seemed frightful enough. I've been walking for hours, trying to find a police station, and I promised James I'd go and see him again and I didn't see how I could get there. My key was in my purse too, and I had to get the caretaker to let me in and he was very grumpy and——'

He pulled up a chair beside her. 'What a long tale of woe! But don't worry, kitten, there's no great harm done.'

'Fifty pounds!' she wailed.

'What's fifty pounds? Think of the National Debt! And we can get the lock changed, to be on the safe side. Did you lose anything else—cheque book? bank card? credit card? passport? No, well, that's all right then, no more to be done. I shouldn't think there's a hope of getting the money back, so we may as well forget about it and turn our thoughts to happier things.'

Amanda dabbed her eyes and tucked her handkerchief into the pocket of her robe. She was suddenly very conscious that she was wearing nothing at all beneath it. Blair hadn't attempted to touch her, but she drew away from him all the same. The closeness of him was having its usual disturbing effect on her body reactions, and if he tried to comfort her—as he might comfort a child—she might lose her head and throw herself into his arms.

She said in a gratifyingly composed voice, 'Terribly sorry to be so feeble, but just for the moment I was at a loss to know what to do. I left my post office book back at Radneys, you see.' She glanced at him and added in a resigned voice, 'But I might have known, mightn't I?'

The dark eyebrows went up. 'Might have known what?'

Her mouth twisted. 'That you'd arrive in time to get me out of a mess. You always do, it seems.'

'I have my uses.' He was laughing openly at her. Then he picked up her left hand, where the diamonds glittered. 'At least you didn't lose this—that *might* have got me worried.' Quite deliberately he bent his head and kissed her fingers one by one, and she felt a tremor run through her.

She pulled her hand away. 'I wish you wouldn't,' she said in a muffled voice.

Dark eyes mocked her. 'A very chaste caress! Surely a fiancé is allowed that much—even in deepest Devon?'.

She couldn't sit beside him any longer. She sprang to her feet, holding the soft, flimsy robe tightly around her. Blair was leaning back in his chair, his long legs stretched out in front of him, studying her with amusement.

'I wish——' she faltered. 'I wish——'

He got slowly to his feet and moved towards her. He was very close now, she could see the tiny lines that fanned out beside his eyes and the way his dark thick brows swept up and outwards and then curved round towards his cheeks; the shadow on his chin and upper lip. She was aware of the masculine smell of him, of his skin, and the fine worsted of his dark grey trousers and lighter jacket.

The smile had gone and there was something in his face now that reminded her of that traumatic experience the first time they met. 'I usually take what I'm offered—if I'm in the mood,' he had drawled contemptuously.

She backed away from him to the bedroom door. With one hand on the knob behind her she heard herself blurt out, 'I just wish you wouldn't keep on making a sort of joke of what we're doing—pretending to be engaged. It makes it all so—so cheap, that's all.'

She just had time to see the look of surprise come into his face before she managed to get herself into the bedroom and close the door. She stood with her back against it, breathing hard.

Well, that was a pathetic sort of outburst, she thought dismally. Now he wouldn't only consider her naïve and ineffective and rather silly, but priggish as well. With a kind of suppressed fury she started to pull on her clothes.

By the time she was dressed she had got control of herself again. Blair was standing by the window looking down when she went back into the sitting room.

'Can we go to the hospital straight away?' she said. 'It may not be too late to see James.'

He turned to face her but didn't move nearer. 'Amanda, I'm sorry,' he said quietly. 'I've been an insensitive oaf. I suppose I had the idea that it might be easier if we made light of this situation.'

She hadn't thought anything could make her feel worse, but this did. She must have given herself away hopelessly. He must know that she was in love with him, and feel sorry for her. She just wanted to sink through the floor.

He took a step towards her, hand outstretched. 'Friends?' he said. 'Friends and partners?'

She put her hand in his; his hand felt hard and cool and his grip was firm and businesslike. 'Yes,' she murmured.

For a moment he held on to her hand, studying her face. Then he gave a small shrug, as if he were shaking off some unwelcome thought, and said, 'Yes, let's go and see how James is getting on.'

It wasn't until a long time later that she realised that never again after that, did he call her 'kitten'.

CHAPTER EIGHT

'GOODNESS, but it's great to be home again!' James sighed contentedly and leaned back against the cushions of the day-bed that had been fixed up for him in his ground-floor study at Radneys. 'I'm not going to relish all this lying about, but it may be tolerable for a while—so long as you promise to come and talk to me now and then, Mandy, and rescue me from the clutches of the good Nurse Phipps.'

Amanda, perched on the end of the bed, a cup of tea in her hand, said anxiously, 'But you like Nurse Phipps, don't you? I thought she seemed rather a dear.'

James looked wry. 'No doubt, but I still prefer my daughter's company.'

'Oh, you'll have plenty of that, I promise you. I shall go and find my way around the mill and the office and then come back and report to you everything that's going on. I'm your personal assistant now, remember?' She smiled at him encouragingly. He looked gaunt and pale, but he had stood the drive home this afternoon, with Fogg behind the wheel of the big limousine, remarkably well.

'Oh—*that*!' he scoffed. 'You'll be a young married woman soon. You won't want to immerse yourself in the business just yet.' Before she could think of a reply to that he went on rather diffidently, 'You know, my dearest girl, I don't want to go on and on about this, but it makes me so happy to know that you're going to marry Blair. Those first days in hospital—it gave me a tremendous lift to know that you were going to be safe and happy. I knew that Blair would never let you down. I used to lie there and picture the future for the two of you. I really believe it saved my

163

life,' he added soberly. 'Where *is* Blair, by the way? Have you seen him today?'

Amanda stood up and carried her cup to the trolley. She could never quite manage to look James straight in the face and talk about Blair. 'No,' she said. 'He said he might be late getting back. Something about setting up a new loom.' It was a relief that Nurse Phipps came in then and the subject of Blair was dropped.

Amanda left James to be 'settled down for a nice rest,' ignoring the face he pulled at her behind the nurse's back, and pushed the tea trolley out to Mrs Fogg. From that lady she heard the excellent news that Mrs French had left the house yesterday.

'And I don't mind telling you now, Miss Dawson, that I was glad to see the last of her.' Mrs Fogg's bright eyes flashed and her rosy cheeks grew still rosier. 'She's not a very nice lady—not very nice at all.' She beamed at Amanda. 'It'll all be much more pleasant now, miss, with you here and getting married to Mr Craddock, and everything.'

Amanda had to put on a performance of a blissfully happy, newly-engaged girl as Mrs Fogg eulogised about Blair and told her how happy they would be, she was sure. And would they be living at Radneys after they were married? It would be so nice if they did, and nice for Mr Dawson too.

Amanda got away as quickly as she could. She would have to put up with a good deal of this as the news got round, she supposed, but she felt a fraud.

She wandered out into the garden, across the lawn, and down the path under the silver birches to the river, where she and Blair had walked together that first night.

Blair, she thought. He was never out of the front of her mind for long, and even when she was trying to think of other things he was still there, as much a part of her as the air she breathed.

Somehow, during these days that had just passed, they had established a kind of working relationship, based on a common aim—to aid James's recovery. Blair had driven up to London every evening, in spite of the pressure of work. Usually he went straight to the hospital and then joined Amanda at the flat for a quick meal before he turned round and drove back again. There was never time to talk much. He began to look very tired as the days went by, but she didn't dare to suggest that he was overdoing it, or that he shouldn't come to London every day. Blair wouldn't take kindly to being mothered, she was sure.

When they did talk it was about James, or about the mill and business generally, just as if he had already accepted her as one of the firm. Once she even plucked up courage to enquire about Juliet and how she was getting on in New York. 'I expect you've heard from her?'

'Juliet?' He looked rather hard at her, but she kept her expression merely friendly and interested. 'Oh yes, she's having a whale of a time, apparently. Says she'll be bursting with new ideas when she gets back again.'

Then he had got to his feet. 'Thanks for the meal, Amanda—must rush away now. I've got hours of work before I get to my bed tonight. See you tomorrow—same time.'

That was how it had been every day. He treated her as a colleague, an equal. He never once teased her, or mocked at her, and he had never once looked at her under those thick dark lashes in a way that made her heart thump against her ribs. She had assured herself that it was better that way. There was no escape for her, because she could never leave James now and she would have to get used to seeing Blair constantly, working with him probably, when the charade of their engagement had been ended. It was better that they should set the pattern for their future relationship now, because somehow she had got to stop loving him.

But at night, when he had gone and she was alone with the aching emptiness inside her, she was afraid that she never would.

Now she came to the end of the path under the silver birches and the river was in front of her. It had been dark that other time when she had stood here with Blair, but today the sunlight sparkled on the clear water as it gurgled over its stones. Darkness then, brightness today. She hoped it was an omen, but she couldn't see how it would work out.

She had been too immersed in her own thoughts to notice the footsteps on the leaf-mould under the trees until a man's voice said, 'Hullo, Amanda.'

She spun round, catching her breath. But it wasn't Blair; to her amazement it was Christopher French who stood before her, smiling his winning smile.

'I brought Mama back to collect the rest of her gear,' he said. 'I couldn't resist coming after you, if only to say goodbye. And to offer my felicitations—I heard about the engagement.'

'Oh,' said Amanda, rather blankly. 'Thank you.'

He leaned back against a tree-trunk, hands in pockets, his light brown eyes twinkling into hers. And again she thought how difficult it was to believe that he was devious and dishonest. He seemed the very picture of an easy-going young man, with his reddish hair and his freckles and his wide, ingenuous grin. Feckless and devil-may-care perhaps, but frank and open, simply because he couldn't be bothered to be anything else. She couldn't help thinking that perhaps James had been a little hard on him.

'So!' He regarded her admiringly as she stood by the river in the light, flowery dress she had bought in London, the magic of the Paris haircut still retaining its shape and framing her small face beguilingly. 'You're even prettier than I remember. I've always had a sneaking admiration for old Blair. He's certainly pulled off the big one this time.'

'What do you mean—the big one?'

He laughed aloud. 'Isn't it obvious, sweetheart? You're certainly worth grabbing, but when Blair gets you he automatically gets the other half of Caradawcs as well—eventually.'

Suddenly she saw Christopher French through James's eyes. Once again her judgment had been at fault. 'That's a rotten thing to say!' she burst out hotly. 'Blair's not that kind of man.'

'Isn't he? I'm afraid I don't believe in the essential goodness of mankind. Everyone for himself is more accurate, I'd say. Not that I blame Blair,' he added frankly. 'I'd have done the same thing myself if you'd given me half a chance. You must have noticed how rapidly I arrived on the scene as soon as Mama tipped me the wink that James's daughter had turned up. But Blair got in first—and I don't argue with a man that's bigger than I am.'

'Oh! I think you're beastly,' Amanda said, disgusted with him now. 'Go away, I don't want to hear any more.' She pushed past him and started to walk quickly back towards the house.

He kept pace with her without effort. 'The one who's lost out seems to be poor Juliet,' he mused. 'I feel sorry for Juliet, she's a nice girl and she's had Blair Craddock in tow for quite some time—ever since he brought her into the firm and fixed a top job for her. I was working there at the time myself and I saw it all going on.' He slid her a meaning glance, which Amanda ignored.

'Still,' he went on, 'maybe it won't cramp his style too much. He's quite a lad, is Blair.'

'Shut up!' snapped Amanda with the utmost fury, and quickened her step until she was nearly running.

She reached the house just as Elaine French came to the front door from the hall, putting two large bags on the step beside her.

'You can put these in the car, Chris,' she said, and turned

to Amanda as he picked up the bags and carried them away
to where his car was standing. She was wearing a tight
black dress today and a lot of gold chains and bracelets.
Her orange hair-do was elaborate and her face a tight mask
that looked as if it might crack at any moment.

'You've come back, have you?' Her voice held its usual
sneer. 'Don't imagine *you've* got rid of me; I just don't
fancy being nursemaid to an invalid, that's all. I have better
things to do with my time.'

Amanda would have gone past her into the house, but it
would have been an undignified scramble to get past Elaine
who was lounging in the doorway, one hand against the
half-open door. The little black eyes looked her up and
down and Elaine said, 'I hear you've caught Blair Craddock. That's a bit of a laugh, isn't it? I suppose you don't
mind that he's had a woman in his apartment all this last
week—that Juliet girl he's been sleeping with for months?
Making the most of their time, no doubt, while the family
was away!' Every word dripped poison.

Amanda could keep silence no longer. She turned on
Mrs French just as she had turned on her son. 'That's a
lie and you know it. Juliet's in New York, she won't be
home for weeks.' Her hand itched to strike the jeering face.

The thin eyebrows rose languidly. 'You poor, stupid
child,' Elaine sneered. 'You're out of your depth here. Why
don't you go back to milking the cows?'

Christopher called, 'All set then—in you get, Mama,'
and his mother teetered down the steps in her absurd heels
and got into the car. Christopher slammed the doors and
lifted a hand in salute. 'Best of luck, sweetheart, if we don't
meet again.' The car rattled away down the drive.

Amanda went into the house and made her way to her
bedroom. Her knees felt weak after that unpleasant encounter. Not that she believed a word of what either of the
Frenches had said. Christopher was just a nasty young
man, trying to score off Blair, against whom he no doubt

bore a grudge—or several of them. But his mother was different. She was really venomous and planted her poison darts where she reckoned they would hurt most. It was just her bad luck, Amanda thought with a small smile, that she didn't know Blair at all.

It was quite unthinkable that Blair should lie to her like that—pretending that he had to rush away from London to catch up on his work. Pretending that he was driving straight to the office to work half the night, when all the time his mistress was here—in his bed—waiting for him.

And anyway, she thought, to clinch the matter finally, why should he have bothered to deceive her? It wasn't as if their engagement was a real engagement, or that he had ever said he loved her. Friends, he had said, and offered her his hand on it.

Something moved in the yard outside the window and she glanced up between the slats of the venetian blind, expecting to see Fogg attending to the big black limousine standing there, the one in which they had driven from London.

But it wasn't Fogg. Someone was coming out of the side door that led to Blair's part of the house. A girl in a silky pale-green suit, carrying a heavy case. Juliet!

She walked to the end garage and opened the doors. Inside stood a small white car which Amanda didn't recognise. Juliet opened the boot and dumped the suitcase inside; backed the car out. Then, in her graceful, unhurried way she went back and closed the garage doors again, climbed into the car, and drove smoothly out of the yard.

Amanda stood quite still, staring out at the now-silent yard where Blair had first come into her life. Elaine had been right, she was out of her depth here. She was living in a world whose values she didn't understand.

There was a knock at the door and Mrs Fogg's neat head appeared. 'I thought you might be here, miss. Mr Dawson has had his rest and he would like to see you. Mr Craddock is with him.'

When she reached the study it was quite a shock to see Blair sitting at ease, laughing with her father. She didn't know what she had expected—that he should look guilty, perhaps, or at least deadly serious.

Her first confused thought, when Mrs Fogg brought the message, was that James must have found out, somehow, what had been going on here in his absence—that the man who was going to marry his daughter had had another woman living here with him—and that some sort of confrontation was about to take place. But evidently not, and that was a relief for James's sake.

Blair jumped to his feet as she came into the room. 'Hullo, darling. I managed to get away early after all.' The same loverlike attitude that he had kept up in London when they had visited the hospital together; the same tenderness in his voice. Then it had seemed all part of the plan they were sharing for James's sake. Now its falseness grated on her nerves, and when his arms came round her and his mouth held hers in a brief but lingering kiss her skin prickled.

Mrs Fogg had been busy turning the study into a comfortable sitting room. A small round table had been set in the window for meals. There were roses on the mahogany desk in the corner, and two of the pale green leather units had been brought in from the drawing room and pushed together to form a small sofa. Blair drew Amanda down on this now, his arm still holding her.

She felt icy cold. It was shock—of course it was. Shock at finding out that Elaine French had been telling her the plain truth and that Blair had lied to her. She sat in the circle of his arm, not really listening as he told James about the new loom that was being installed at the mill, and tried to convince herself that his deceit had been the worst thing.

But she knew that wasn't quite true. The very worst

thing, that was giving her this sick, empty feeling, was that he and Juliet had been here together every night, while she was alone in London. Here together—making love—jealousy gnawed with sharp teeth and she shivered suddenly.

'Cold, dear?' Blair stopped in the middle of what he was saying to James to regard her lovingly.

Dear! How cosy! How domestic! He was a splendid actor, it must come naturally to him, she thought bitterly.

'No, not really.' She couldn't look at him. 'Just a bit tired, perhaps.' Gran would have added, 'Someone walking over my grave.' And that was exactly how it felt.

James regarded her pale face anxiously. 'You look all in, Mandy. You must have an early night. I'm afraid I've been a nuisance to everybody lately, but I promise to do better in future. Now, what do you think—would a month be long enough for you?'

She had lost track of the conversation. 'A month?' she echoed. 'What for?'

Blair's arm tightened round her with a quick, warning pressure. 'For our wedding, of course, muggins,' he teased. 'It seems James has been planning in secret. Village wedding, simple ceremony, flowers, organ music. The bride, all in white, looking——' the laughter went out of his voice as he tipped up her face to his. '—looking just what she is, the most wonderful girl in the world.' His eyes adored her, his deep voice even held an authentic throb of passion.

She didn't think she could take much more or she would start to hate him. She laughed lightly and wriggled out of his arms. 'What a pretty picture! But I'm afraid the stage-managing would take more than a month.' She crossed the room and sat on the edge of James's day-bed. 'We must wait for you to get quite fit again.'

He took her hand in his and patted it, giving her his monkey smile. 'Nothing like a wedding to speed on the repair process,' he told her. 'Now I know you two must want to be on your own. Go along out into the garden while I have my supper—' as Nurse Phipps came in bearing a tray. 'Come and say goodnight to me, Amanda?'

The long window was open. They walked across the lawn and under the archway of laurel that led to the river path. When they were out of sight of the house Amanda drew away and said coolly, 'We don't need to keep up the play-acting now. And I'd like to go in—I can keep out of James's sight if I go round the front way.'

He put a hand on her arm. 'You really are tired, aren't you?' His voice was concerned. Perhaps he *was* feeling badly about the way he had deceived her. 'But walk down to the river with me first.'

'No, I don't think so. I——'

'Please, Amanda. There's something I want to say to you.'

To explain about Juliet? That might make it easier to bear. If he told her himself it might mean that they could still be friends. 'All right,' she agreed, and fell into step again beside him, keeping a little distance between them.

The wind had got up with the coming of the dusk and the leaves of the silver birch trees rustled in the suddenly chilly air. The river looked grey and sombre now and there were dark shadows beneath the overhanging branches.

Blair stood staring down at the moving water, frowning, hands deep in his pockets. She felt almost sorry for him. It wouldn't be easy for a man like this to acknowledge that he had behaved less than honourably.

Just when she felt she couldn't bear the silence any longer he drew in a sharp breath and said, 'Amanda, will you marry me? And this time—as they say—it's for real.'

Her mind went blank. 'Did you—did you say marry you?'

'Yes.' He glanced at her startled face and looked away again. 'I didn't mean to ask you yet, but James has rather brought matters to a head with his plans for speeding up the wedding. All the time we've been in London I've been planning how best to say this and now I'm afraid I haven't done it too well. But will you think about it, Amanda? I believe we could make it work.'

She walked away from him, nearer to the river. *All the time we've been in London,* he had said. It was like dreaming a nightmare and then waking up to find it coming true. Elaine had been right. Christopher had been right. And Blair Craddock belonged to their sophisticated, cynical world; a world where a man would marry for personal gain and keep a mistress on the side; a world that she didn't understand and wanted no part of.

But in the nightmare there was one thing that she clung on to: somehow she must keep control. There must be no emotional outburst, no accusations, no stressful situation created for James.

Blair's voice came from behind her. 'Well, what do you think?'

Think? She couldn't think at all. She put a hand to her temple where a pulse was throbbing and said the first thing that came into her mind. 'I'm sorry, Blair, but it wouldn't be any good.'

He said quickly, 'Is it the career thing you were talking about in London? Are you really sold on that? Because if you are, that would be there too, if you wanted. I wasn't suggesting a slippers-by-the-fire marriage. We'd be partners, Amanda. We could make a go of it.'

His voice was urgent now and he had moved closer. Through the thin stuff of her dress she felt his hand at her waist. 'Don't touch me!' she said sharply, moving away.

But that was too emotional. At all costs she must avoid a scene. For James's sake this 'engagement' had to go on for a little longer. She looked down into the river and said in a muffled voice, 'I'm sorry, Blair, but I—I *couldn't.*'

As soon as she had said the words she realised with

horror exactly what they must mean to him—to any man—
and she would have taken them back if she could have
done. She stood, miserably clenching her hands, while the
long silence became more and more unbearable.

At last he said in a voice completely without expression, 'I see. Well, you don't have to apologise. I thought—
but never mind that now. May I assume you're still willing to go on with our—pretence until James is in the clear?
It may be several weeks. Can you bear it as long as that?'

It was mortifying how something inside her insisted on
aching for his hurt masculine pride. She whispered, 'Oh
yes. I promised I would.'

'Good.' He was brisk and businesslike now. 'I'll make it
as easy as I can for you. I'm afraid I didn't realise how you
felt or I would have been more careful not to embarrass
you. I'll keep out of your way as far as possible, of course,
without raising doubts in James's mind.'

Oh God, she thought desperately, I can't take much
more of this. 'I expect we'll manage,' she said tonelessly. 'I
think I'll go in now; it looks as if it might rain.'

He glanced up vaguely at the darkening sky between the
branches. 'I won't come with you. Tell James I've had to
go back to the mill. Tell him——' He stopped suddenly
and she saw the way his anger exploded, snapping his control. 'Oh, tell him what the hell you like!' he shouted, like
a man at the end of his tether, and strode off along the
path, the dead twigs cracking under his feet.

'Your breakfast, miss.' Mrs Fogg put down the tray. 'And
a letter for you.'

Amanda heard the words through a thick blanket of
sleep. There had been a thunderstorm in the night and she
had spent the greater part of it sitting in a chair, because
that seemed easier than lying down trying to persuade
herself that she could go to sleep. It wasn't any good trying
to think, either, because her head felt as if it were held in

an iron vice and the thoughts churned about in it chaotic-
ally as the wind screamed and the rain beat against the
window. But towards dawn the storm had passed and she
had undressed and crawled into bed and slept heavily.

'Did the storm bother you in the night, miss? It was
quite nasty, but everything looks nice and fresh this morning.' Mrs Fogg pulled back the curtains and adjusted the
venetian blind so that the sun threw bars of yellow light
across the room. 'There, I'll leave you to have your breakfast.'

With an enormous effort Amanda pulled herself up, running her fingers through her mane of fair hair. The coffee
smelt good and she poured out a cup and wakened herself
up with it while she read her letter.

It was from King's Holton, from Mrs Grose, the post-
mistress, who had been a friend of Gran's. She was pleased
to have Amanda's letter, she wrote, and to hear that she
was staying with her father for a while. 'Your Gran told
me a bit about how family things have been in the past,' the
letter went on, 'but I'm sure she would have wished to let
bygones be bygones.' There followed some items of village
news and messages from friends who all wanted to know
why she had disappeared so suddenly and when she was
coming back.

'I look forward to seeing you before long,' Mrs Grose
concluded. 'The solicitor from Exeter came down yesterday to look at your Gran's cottage and he left a key with
me as he's a little worried about some damp in one of the
walls and asked me to keep an eye on things, but I should
feel easier in my mind if you could see it for yourself.' She
remained, Yours affectionately, Freda Grose.

Amanda was suddenly drowned in homesickness. She
had hardly had time to think of King's Holton since she left
it, but the letter had brought it all back, and the longing
to see it again, to be among her friends, was like a giant
hand squeezing her, deep inside.

If she showed the letter to James and explained that she thought she should go to the cottage to see what the trouble was with the wall, he would try to dissuade her, would tell her that the solicitors would take care of everything. But if she insisted? If she told him she would really like to go—that there were personal things she would like to have with her—surely, then, he would agree? Just for one night, she would say, then I'll be back with you again.

But would she? Once she got back to the cottage, to the people she understood and felt easy with, would she have the strength of will to come back? Come back to face weeks of seeing Blair every day, to keep up the pretence of being engaged, to let him touch her, kiss her?

She stared out of the window, remembering how she had first seen him there, getting out of his car—the man in the background. In the background, that was a laugh. He was right here, in her heart and her body. Perhaps she should feel ashamed that she still loved him, ached for him, whatever he had done, whatever sort of man he was, but she didn't feel ashamed. The longing was there, dragging at her, however she might try to deny it.

Then—to get right away?

You promised, a small voice inside told her. You promised James, you promised Blair.

She thrust Mrs Grose's letter back into its envelope and finished her coffee. Then she got out of bed and made her way to the bathroom to shower. She would just have to face whatever the day brought. It was inconvenient to have a conscience, but if you'd been brought up that way, she thought wryly, you were stuck with it, and that was that. She would have to see it through.

The worst thing was not knowing when she would have to face Blair again and how he would behave. Her knees still felt weak when she remembered the sudden blaze of anger in his face last night.

She lingered over dressing, hoping that she would catch

a glimpse of his car leaving for the mill, and know that he was off the premises and that she had a respite. But the shiny blue garage doors were closed and the yard remained empty and silent in the sunshine.

At last she couldn't stay in her room any longer. Walking down the corridor she encountered Nurse Phipps tiptoeing out of James's bedroom. When she saw Amanda she put a finger to her lips. 'Still sleeping,' she announced with satisfaction. 'Do him the world of good after the journey yesterday. Lovely day, isn't it, Miss Dawson? We'll be able to get your father out to sit in the garden later on.'

'Yes,' said Amanda politely. 'That will be splendid.'

She went out of the house through the garden-room door and round the end of the wing to the garage yard. Fogg was here now, tending the big black limousine.

'Morning, miss. Lovely day.'

'Yes, isn't it?' Everyone thought it was a lovely day, so she supposed it must be. 'Has Mr Craddock left yet?'

The chauffeur glanced up quickly at her. 'Mr Craddock wasn't at home last night, miss.' He wouldn't show any surprise at the question, he was too well trained for that. But a girl would be expected to know her fiancé's plans. She must be more careful.

'Oh yes, of course,' she said brightly. 'I'd forgotten.' She walked away before her face could betray her. Of course—Blair would have been wherever Juliet was. Juliet had left here and he had gone after her.

The hours crawled past. Amanda wandered round the gardens, avoiding the river path as if it were inhabited by dangerous beasts. She looked in to see her father when he wakened. On Nurse Phipps' orders he stayed in bed until after lunch and Amanda ate her lunch on the terrace, with the tinted roof throwing a green shade over her. It was very peaceful, very quiet. Nothing to do but think, and her thoughts were painful.

A lovely day! A day for lovers; a day to wander into the

woods, arms entwined, with the call of wood-pigeons and the musky scent of leaf-mould; a day to lie together by the river with its lazy gurgle in your ears. Stop it, Amanda, she ordered herself.

Later, James got up and dressed and was established on a lounger in the shade of a huge copper beech. Amanda sat on the grass beside him and they talked about the house and how they would rearrange it. 'It'll all be better now that Elaine has taken herself off,' he mused with satisfaction. 'You can have a free hand to make it over, my dear. I was wondering if it would be a good idea if we changed round, when you and Blair are married. Perhaps I could take over his wing of the house and you two could make the main part your home. That is, if you won't mind having your old dad around the place?' he added with mock pathos.

It should have been heaven, out here in the cool shade of the beech tree, with the lazy buzzing of bees and the scent of roses in the air. Mrs Fogg brought out a tray and Amanda poured tea and they ate her special tiny iced cakes.

Sometimes they talked, sometimes James closed his eyes and lay back in his chair with an apologetic grin. And all the time Amanda listened tensely for the sound of a car coming up the drive beyond the laurels and wondered nervously what would happen when Blair came home. If they met in James's presence he would have to keep up the play-acting. He would put his arms round her and kiss her and she didn't know how she was going to bear it. Perhaps it would be better if James were persuaded to go back into the house and then she could sit in her bedroom and watch for Blair's car returning to the garage, so that their meeting could be in private.

But before she could put her plan into action she heard a car coming up the drive and her inside gave an unpleasant jolt. James opened his eyes. 'There's Blair now,' he said, and added with a twinkle, 'Run and meet him.'

She scrambled to her feet and was halfway across the lawn before she saw that it wasn't Blair, rounding the corner of the laurel hedge and coming towards her. It was Juliet, exquisite as ever in a tailored sleeveless dress of amber silk, sensible enough to wear at work but infinitely becoming, with her creamy skin and wallflower brown eyes.

Her face lit up as she saw Amanda. She took both her hands and kissed her. 'My dear,' she said, 'I was so thrilled to hear about you and Blair. I think it's just perfect, and I hope you'll be terribly happy.'

They were within earshot of James, so of course she had to say that, but how sincere it sounded! How radiantly happy she looked herself! But of course she would, wouldn't she? By now Blair would have told her that Amanda was laying no claim, that she had refused to marry him.

Juliet went and leaned over James's chair and kissed him. 'Dear James, you gave us all such a turn, you wretch. But you look fine now, much better than I expected. Did you get my super get-well cards when you were in hospital?'

'I did indeed,' James said, smiling up at her affectionately. 'And the flowers. Very much appreciated.'

'Good. I'd have liked to come and see you, but I knew you had Amanda, and'—she gave a crooked little smile— 'things were rather fraught here when I got back from New York.'

James nodded understandingly. 'I can well believe that— but all's well now?'

'Blissfully, unbelievably well. I'm re-born. It's been a wonderful week. Blair lent us his apartment, did he tell you? He's been sleeping at the office, poor lamb, but he said it didn't matter because he was madly busy all the time he was commuting to London each day.' She turned and glanced at Amanda and then back to James. 'Does Amanda know—about my grisly story?'

He shook his head. 'Not from me. I left it to you or Blair.'

'*Has* Blair told you, Amanda? No, I can see he hasn't. You tell her, James, she's one of us now.' She beamed at them both. 'I must fly now, I'm on my way to the station to track down a package that hasn't turned up. But we'll all meet again soon and have a lovely time. Look after yourself, James.' She patted his cheek, smiled at Amanda and ran off across the lawn, stopping on the way to turn and call back to them, 'Blair says he may be late home—*work*!'

Amanda stared after her blankly, her mind in turmoil. She sank down on the rug and looked up at James pleadingly. 'What was that all about?'

James gazed ahead of him, down the length of the garden. 'Poor Juliet, she's a grand kid. How she's kept so cheerful these last two years——' He transferred his look to Amanda. 'She's married, you know, to a fellow called Rayne—Giles Rayne. I'd never heard of him until Blair told me about it a few days ago. I'd always imagined that she and Blair would link up some time or other. It just shows how wrong you can be.'

'Yes,' whispered Amanda. She was just beginning to glimpse the depths of her own error and what she saw appalled her. 'Tell me,' she said.

'I don't know all the details, but it seems that Blair had known the two of them when they were all students together at art college. A couple of years ago he ran into Juliet in London and she was in the depths of despair. She had just married this Giles and they had gone abroad for their honeymoon—rather unwisely, I'd think, to a country whose ideas don't exactly fit in with ours. Even more unwisely Giles, who's a photographer, had been taking pictures quite innocently near a lake. It was his bad luck that there happened to be some hush-hush establishment in the trees around same lake.' James glanced at Amanda with a shrug. 'If you read your papers you can guess what happened next. They were pounced upon and stuck in prison.'

'Oh,' she breathed, forgetting all about her personal problem. 'How awful!'

'Yes, I gather it was rather bad. After some time they let Juliet go and escorted her out of the country. But her husband has been held ever since, until last week.'

'So Blair helped Juliet—brought her here—gave her a job——?' It was beginning to make sense now.

James nodded. 'They were his friends; he's very loyal, is Blair. Juliet asked him to tell nobody, not even me. She was sensitive about it getting into the papers, having reporters milling around, everyone asking questions and pitying her. She knew everything was being done, through official channels, and she just had to wait and put a good face on it. She's been rather super, I think. Then when she was in New York, she heard that Giles had been released at last and she flew back immediately and—well, that's the story. Happy ending!'

'Yes, happy ending indeed. I'm so glad for them,' sighed Amanda. And knew that she was.

Across the dark countryside came the sound of the clock in the village church striking twelve and still Blair hadn't returned. Amanda prowled restlessly about her bedroom, sitting down, getting up again, peering through the slats in the venetian blinds at Blair's apartment in the opposite wing. She had had her dinner in here and she had been here ever since, so that she would know the minute he came in. Dreading it too, but resolved that before the night was out she must see him to try to put things right between them, to explain somehow what had happened, why she had believed what she had about him.

She stared into the darkness of the garage area outside the window. He couldn't have come in without her hearing his car, seeing the lights. Perhaps he was sleeping at the office again tonight, staying there to work off his anger. She shivered as she remembered the expression on his face when he had swung away from her down by the river yesterday.

The sensible thing to do would be to switch on the light and draw the curtains and go to bed, but she was past doing anything sensible. She had to see him to tell him she was sorry. She couldn't sleep until she had at least done that, so she had to wait.

Another half hour crawled past. Then, when she had almost given up hope, there was the sound of a car in the distance, coming up the drive. Lights flickered, and then flared outside the window, throwing white bars through the venetian blind on to the walls and floor. She held her breath, as if Blair could possibly see her, cowering here in the darkness.

The car slid to a halt, the purr of the engine shut off and she could just make out the shape of Blair's tall form as he got out of the car. His footsteps sounded on the paved yard, dragging a little as if he were desperately tired. The door to his apartment opened, closed. Inside, a light came on in one of the windows.

Amanda drew in a couple of deep breaths. She must get it over quickly. Her inside felt quite hollow as she stole down the quiet corridor, through the door in the garden room and around to the side door of Blair's apartment. She knocked and waited. The night was warm, but her hands were clammy cold and she was shivering.

The door opened a little way and the light from inside almost blinded her. She had been so long in the dark. Blair exclaimed, 'Amanda! What the blazes do you want here at this time of night?'

It wasn't encouraging. She faltered, 'May I speak to you—*please*.'

He opened the door wider. 'Well—you'd better come in.'

She followed him into the book-lined sitting room. He

went straight across and poured himself a drink. He said curtly, 'It's late and I'm very tired. Please say what you have to say and go.'

She saw how pale and drawn his face was, the deep lines from nose to mouth exaggerated. Almost her courage failed her, but she was here now and she had to try. She said, 'Just that—I'm sorry about what I said to you last night. I didn't mean it in—in the way you thought.'

He made an irritated, dismissive gesture. 'Isn't this all rather a waste of time?'

'It isn't to me,' she said, more steadily now.

He came slowly across the room, glass in hand, eyeing her warily. 'What exactly are you trying to tell me?'

Suddenly all her careful explanations, the words she had been rehearsing as she waited in her room, went out of her head. She only knew she loved him desperately and that if he didn't love her and want her, nothing really mattered. For perhaps the first time in her life, as she looked into his eyes, she was fully conscious of herself as a woman.

Then, quite deliberately, she smiled at him.

He stared at her like a man who only half believes what he is seeing. He put both hands on her shoulders and a shudder ran through her. 'Amanda?' he said huskily.

She went into his arms, linking her fingers behind his head, her lips parting to invite his kiss, her body pressing softly against his own. She saw his eyes near to hers, burning with dark blue fire, but she didn't close her own eyes. His arms went round her hungrily, as if he would merge their two bodies into one, and she heard his breathing, as quick and uneven as her own; felt him trembling against her.

Then, his tiredness gone, he picked her up in his arms. She clung to him, her arms round his neck, her face against his shoulder.

He said urgently, 'I hope to God, Amanda, that you know what you're doing this time.'

'Yes,' she murmured, still smiling. 'Oh, yes!'

Amanda opened her eyes and it was early morning. Through the window she saw that the sky was pearly grey, suffused with the pink of sunrise. She drew in a deep breath. There was no slow dragging back to consciousness today; it was all there immediately—the joy, the gentleness, the passion, the *rightness*.

There was a gentle knock on the door. Then Blair came in, balancing a mug, which he put down beside her. He was dressed and shaved. His dark hair was brushed. He looked fabulous, thought Amanda, letting her gaze rest on him luxuriously.

'Your tea, madame.' He stood looking down at her and their eyes met and held, remembering, and it was as if they were making love.

Then he straightened his shoulders and retired to the far end of the room. He stood with his arms folded, eyeing her with frank delight as she sat up and reached for the mug of tea. 'I think,' he said reluctantly, 'that it might be advisable to cover up.' He took her dressing gown from a chair and tossed it across the room to her. 'Otherwise——' he drawled the word significantly, his eyes loving her, 'I shall never get as far as my car, let alone all the way to London.'

She slipped her arms into the gown. 'London?' she wailed. 'Must you go to London—today?'

'Yes, I must, my darling,' he said firmly. 'To make arrangements for our marriage at the earliest moment. Tomorrow, if it's possible. James will have to wait a little longer for his pretty village wedding, with all the trimmings. I,' he added in a suddenly shaken voice, 'can't wait to put my ring on your finger.'

He came across the room and stopped a little way from her. 'Why?' he said slowly. '*Why*, Amanda?'

She knew what he was asking. She searched her mind

for all the doubts and miseries that had been crowded together there only yesterday, and could find nothing but shadowy traces.

She frowned a little. 'I thought you were in love with Juliet,' she said. 'You see, I didn't know until yesterday what—what her position was. She was so lovely, so much part of your world, and I felt so young and silly and naïve. So—so inadequate.'

'Inadequate!' His voice, his eyes, mocked her softly and a bright flush came to her cheeks.

'Well, I did,' she insisted. 'And when you asked me to marry you I thought it was just—just for the sake of the firm. You know—linking the two royal houses together. Craddock and Dawson—Caradawc,' she added, inspired.

He gave a shout of laughter. 'It's not such a bad idea at that. I wish I'd thought of it myself. But didn't you guess I was in love with you? I'd have thought it stuck out all over me.'

She shook her head. 'You treated me like a child.'

'I think I had to. Those evenings in London—I had to rush away to stop myself going overboard and spoiling my chances with you for good. You see, my love, I thought I'd frightened you pretty badly that first evening of Elaine's awful party. I wanted to wait, to give you time to trust me. I was scared that you never would.'

'You only had to tell me you loved me.'

He smiled. 'And you, my dearest girl, had only to give me a bit of encouragement.'

'Encouragement? *You?*' she scoffed.

'Indeed. I was scared stiff. You can be very off-putting with that straight gaze of yours, and you went to the trouble of assuring me that you were a career girl and you weren't in love with anyone. Cool, that's what you were.'

She said, 'I don't think I'm a career girl, though I'd like to be involved where I can help. And'—she met his look with a rueful lift of her eyebrows—'I'm not really cool either.'

'Thank God,' he said fervently, and they both laughed.

He dropped to his knees beside the bed. 'I've got to leave you now, beloved. He leaned towards her and for a brief moment his mouth was pressed hard against hers while his hands were strong and warm on her soft flesh beneath the loose covering of her dressing gown.

They clung together desperately, their need almost overwhelming. Then Blair drew away and stood up. 'I'm going,' he said shakily. 'I'll stay in London tonight—it'll be easier that way. I'll phone you when I've got things fixed up.'

He walked to the door and stood there, gazing at her. 'I can't believe it's true,' he said wonderingly, and went out.

Amanda sat biting her knuckles. She heard the car door slam, the roar of the powerful engine as it fired. She slid out of the bed, pulling the dressing gown round her and stumbled across to the window.

A cold, early-morning breeze stung her hot cheeks. Blair was at the wheel of the car across the yard, his hand on the gear lever, the engine ticking over sweetly. He wound down the window as he saw her. 'Want me?'

She lifted a hand. 'Just—take care—come home safe.'

He grinned back at her, his dark eyes brilliant. 'You bet!' he called back, and let in the clutch.

She waited until she could no longer hear the sound of the car in the clear cold morning air. Then, with a smile hovering on her mouth and her eyes dreamy, she began to count the moment until she was in his arms again.

Harlequin Salutes...

Rachel Lindsay

CAGE OF GOLD
HOUSE OF LORRAINE
THE TAMING OF LAURA
PRINCE FOR SALE
SECRETARY WIFE
ALIEN CORN

Six best-selling Harlequin books
by a world-famous author.

Each volume, attractively bound in
a uniquely designed cover, is a warm
and moving love story—the sort of story
that only an author as sensitive and
imaginative as Rachel Lindsay can produce.

Look for these beautiful books in June
at your favorite store.

What the press says about Harlequin romance fiction...

"The most popular reading matter of American women today."
— *The Detroit News*

"Women have come to trust these stories about contemporary people, set in exciting foreign places."
— *Best Sellers*, New York

"Harlequin novels have a vast and loyal readership."
— *Toronto Star*

Get all the latest books before they're sold out!

As a Harlequin subscriber you actually receive your personal copies of the latest Romances immediately after they come off the press, so you're sure of getting all 6 each month.

Cancel your subscription whenever you wish!

You don't have to buy any minimum number of books. Whenever you decide to stop your subscription just let us know and we'll cancel all further shipments.

Your FREE gift includes

- *Anne Hampson* — Beyond the Sweet Waters
- *Anne Mather* — The Arrogant Duke
- *Violet Winspear* — Cap Flamingo
- *Nerina Hilliard* — Teachers Must Learn